Pushing Past the Pain

An inspirational romance

Milla Holt

Reinbok Limited

LONDON, UNITED KINGDOM

Published by Reinbok Limited
Kemp House,
152 – 160 City Road,
London EC1V 2NX

Book Layout © 2017 BookDesignTemplates.com
Cover by 100Covers
Editing by Krista Wagner

Pushing Past the Pain/ Milla Holt. -- 1st ed.
ISBN 978-1-913416-03-4

To my husband, who is my biggest
cheerleader,
and my amazing beta readers
Marvi, Donna, and Elizabeth

contents

Chapter One

ELLA BELMONT TOOK one look at her mother-in-law's puffy face and red-rimmed eyes and knew she'd have to postpone her trip to the grocery store. Jocelyn Belmont stood on the front doorstep, clutching a large cardboard box.

"Come in," Ella said, stepping back. She ought to have guessed the older woman might need a shoulder to cry on, given what the date was today.

Jocelyn walked into the entryway. The box rattled as she raised it toward Ella. "I was going through some things in the garage and I found these. They were part of Neil's old Lego collection. I thought Tiffany might want them." She thrust the box into Ella's hands. "I hope you're doing okay, hun," she said, her voice trembling.

"Yes, thanks," Ella said. "How are you holding up?"

Jocelyn sighed and dabbed her eyes with a balled-up tissue. "It's hard. His birthdays always get to me."

"I know," Ella said. She set the box on the floor and drew Jocelyn into a hug.

Ella's husband, Neil, would have been turning thirty-five next week, if he had still been alive. Jocelyn had been devastated by the death of her only son and found birthdays particularly hard to cope with. Ella dealt with Neil's birthdays the same way she handled every other milestone since his death: by stuffing her feelings deep inside and pretending it was just another day.

"Can I get you anything? A cup of tea?" Ella asked. Jocelyn was a talker, and Ella knew that the best way to get her through any rough patch was to let her talk through it. The two women had shared many tea and chatting sessions over the past couple of years.

"Yes, please," Jocelyn said, walking into the open plan living room of Ella's basement apartment. "Where's Tiffany?"

Ella pointed to the French doors that led out into the back yard. "She's playing out there."

Jocelyn moved toward the doors while Ella put the kettle on. "She looks more like him every day." Jocelyn wiped at a fresh trickle of tears.

Ella followed the older woman's gaze to her five-year-old daughter who sat cross-legged on a picnic rug, a collection of toys strewn around her. Jocelyn had always been adamant that the child looked like Neil, but Ella had never thought so, and she didn't see it now.

Tiffany had inherited her mother's dark brown eyes, oval face, and firm round chin. Her tawny skin was a blend of her father's fair tones and her mother's mahogany complexion. Tiffany's curly brown hair hung down her back in two pigtails. It, too, lay on the spectrum between her mother's tight black Afro curls and her father's wavy blond hair. But Jocelyn saw her son in the little girl, and Ella didn't want to contradict her.

The kettle whistled, and Ella went to fetch two mugs from the cupboard. Milk and one sugar for Jocelyn, milk and two sugars for herself. Jocelyn turned around and came to the kitchen counter, perching herself onto a bar stool. She curled her fingers around the mug that Ella slid toward her.

"Thanks, love," Jocelyn said, blowing on the top of the steaming drink. "It's good to have you two so close by. Especially on days like today."

Ella smiled and nodded. It was indeed a blessing to be able to stay in this apartment, a self-contained granny annex attached to Jocelyn's house. After Neil died, Ella couldn't keep up the mortgage on their four-bed family home in Reigate, an exclusive neighborhood of Surrey, England. It had been a stretch even while Neil was alive, but he had insisted on living in that area. With him gone, there was no way she could afford to stay on.

After the burial, Jocelyn had urged Ella and Tiffany to stay in her basement apartment and lease out the Reigate house. The rental income from Ella's family home was supposed to cover the mortgage. It was a good idea in theory, but it hadn't worked out that smoothly, particularly with her current set of tenants.

As much as Ella was grateful to Jocelyn for giving her and Tiffany a roof over their heads, living so close to Neil's mother had its drawbacks as well as its advantages.

She envied Jocelyn's pure grief for her son. Her mother-in-law was able to mourn over Neil's best qualities: his spontaneity, his infectious grin, his ability to cram fun and laughter into every corner of his life. While Ella missed that part of her husband, she couldn't forget the darker side of his live-for-the-moment outlook. Her grief was stained with ugly memories and the very real implications of the situation his hedonism had left her and her daughter in.

Jocelyn sipped her tea. "You know, I was thinking," she said. "Neil was taken away from us far too soon. But I'm thankful for how much he packed into his short time with us. He really lived his life to the full, didn't he? He went after everything he wanted. He grabbed life by the horns and gave it a good shake." She smiled, despite the tears that welled up in her eyes, and reached out to grab Ella's hand. "That's what gives me the most comfort when I'm feeling at my lowest. He made the most of his time."

Ella stretched her lips into the semblance of a smile but could not muster any words in response. Neil had certainly gone after everything he wanted, seldom thinking about the consequences. As his widow with a young child to raise, she saw things rather differently than his indulgent mother, to whom he had always been a golden boy, entitled to whatever wish crossed his fancy. Neil had gone off on that lads-only holiday in Hawaii to celebrate his friend's upcoming wedding even though Ella tried to reason with him that they couldn't afford it. He'd waved a shiny new credit card at her and said, "Yes, we can."

He and his friends had the time of their lives, enjoying Maui to the full, culminating in a skydiving trip that had gone terribly wrong.

"It always makes me feel better knowing that he died doing something he loved," Jocelyn continued, squeezing Ella's hand.

Ella clenched her jaw. Neil might have loved skydiving, but their insurance company didn't. They'd used it as an excuse to deny both his travel insurance and his term life policies. "Void when the policyholder dies in pursuit of dangerous activities." Ella was grateful that she had joint ownership of the Reigate property, which meant that it had passed on to her. Otherwise, it would have been counted as Neil's estate and sucked into the black hole of his massive personal debts.

She couldn't join in on Jocelyn's celebration of Neil's short-sighted pleasure-seeking. Tears stung her eyes, and she stood up and walked to the window to watch her daughter. Tiffany was Neil's best gift to her. For her child, she could almost forgive Neil for everything he'd put her through over the years. Almost.

Jocelyn came up to the window as well, and Tiffany looked up and saw them both. She grinned, displaying the new gap where she'd just lost her first baby tooth. Mother and grandmother smiled and waved back, and Jocelyn sighed. "It's wonderful having you both so close."

"We're grateful to be here, too," Ella said, glad she could return her mother-in-law's sincerity on this point at least.

Jocelyn turned to face her. "I wanted to have a special dinner next week to mark Neil's birthday. I thought about doing it last year, but I just couldn't. It was all too fresh. I'll cook all his favorite things, and we can light a candle and just remember him. It'll be just us."

Ella knew that it wasn't a question. Jocelyn was laying out how she and, therefore, Ella and Tiffany, would be celebrating Neil's birthday. Jocelyn expected everyone else who loved Neil to feel the same way she did. It had been like that since Neil had gone. Jocelyn was the chief mourner, and everyone else followed her impulses and ideas of how things would be done. In the early days, when numbness and shock paralyzed Ella's thoughts and feelings, she had done everything according to Jocelyn's wishes. The pattern was now fixed in stone and impossible to break. Jocelyn, in her sweet-natured yet single-minded way, dictated what was to be done and how Neil was to be grieved.

Ella said, "Yes, we'll be there. Just let us know the time."

"Thanks, darling," Jocelyn said, squeezing Ella's hand. "It'll be hard, but it's such a comfort to have each other. I'd better go now. Don't forget to show Tiffany the Legos and tell her where they came from. I might drop by tomorrow and have a little play with her. See you soon."

Ella watched as Jocelyn headed to the front door and let herself out. She opened the door to the back yard and called out to her daughter. "Tiffany, let's go. We need to get some groceries."

Chapter Two

RAGNAR KLASSEN READ from the grocery list in his hand. "Laundry soap," he muttered, pushing his shopping cart down the aisle of the Tesco Superstore. He glanced at his daughter Sophie, who walked beside him with her stuffed rabbit, Clump, tucked under her arm.

That rabbit had seen a lot. Along with him and his daughter, it had spent the last year traveling in Europe, Africa, and Australia. Now it had come full circle and was back in the village of Hatbrook in southeast England, browsing the shelves of the same Tesco Superstore where a young mother had once pulled the stuffed rabbit off the shelf on impulse, liking its lopsided ears and thinking it would look sweet in her baby daughter's nursery. That mother was gone now, mowed down by a hit-and-run driver, and the husband and daughter she had left behind were trying to get their groceries and cobble together the pieces of their shattered life.

Sophie rubbed the rabbit's paw between her forefinger and thumb, a gesture fixed from long habit, and which contributed to Clump's almost furless state.

"We just need to get some washing soap and a couple of other things, then we'll be done," Ragnar said. They went to the laundry aisle, and he stood looking at the ridiculous array of soaps. The smells of several dozen detergents assailed his nose. Which one should he get?

It had been well over a year since he'd been shopping in an English grocery store. He couldn't remember the name of the brand Zuri had liked, the one which made all their clothes smell like fresh air blowing through the window on a sunny spring morning.

He picked up a bottle for a closer look. Non-bio detergent. What on earth was non-bio? Was that a good thing? He decided to go for it. And should he get it in liquid or powder form? There were laundry pods as well. He had never tried those before. One pod per wash. That looked simple; it meant he wouldn't have to worry about measuring it out. Pods it was; he could tick that off his list.

All that was left was shampoo. That should be on the next aisle. "Almost done, sweetheart," he said to Sophie, although she wasn't showing the slightest sign of impatience. He was the one who was sick of shopping and wanted to get back home. No, he didn't just want to go home. What he wanted most of all was to get into a time machine and magically appear back in the past when Zuri was here, not just to tell him what detergent and shampoo they should use, but to laugh with him and fill his arms as well as his heart.

Ragnar and Sophie walked into the personal hygiene aisle, steering the large shopping cart around a woman and child who stood browsing the shower gels. "Shampoo, shampoo, shampoo," he said under his breath. He scoured the shelves but couldn't find the kind Zuri had used for Sophie. He'd have to get an alternative. Once again, there were too many to choose from. Why did they make so many kinds? He headed closer to the shelves where the bottles featured glossy-haired models.

"For colored hair." No, that wouldn't do. "Heat-damaged hair." "Tames frizz." "Ultimate detangling conditioning shampoo." He glanced at his daughter's thick mop of hair, then back at the bottle. This might be worth a try. He turned to drop the bottle into the cart.

"Is that for your daughter? I wouldn't use that."

Ragnar glanced up. The woman he'd seen in the aisle before was standing a few feet away, one hand on her own shopping cart. Her other hand pointed at Ragnar's bottle.

"I shouldn't buy this?" he asked. "Why not?"

The woman said, "It's loaded with sulfates. That's the worst thing for curly hair. It'll strip out any natural moisture and leave the hair brittle and make the tangles worse. You want to look for something that's based on natural ingredients and try to avoid sulfates completely."

Ragnar gave his self-appointed consultant a double take. Her black hair was short, its tight ringlets framing her oval face. It looked simple, but very attractive. He glanced at the little girl with her, who was about Sophie's age. While the woman was as dark as Zuri, her daughter was clearly mixed race. But unlike Sophie's unruly curls, this child had perfectly groomed pigtails secured with tiny bows. Judging from the look of this woman and her child, Ragnar was convinced that she knew about hair.

"Thanks for the advice," he said. "Which one should I get?"

The woman shrugged a slender shoulder. "To be honest, Tesco doesn't have our favorite products, but you could do a lot worse than this one if you're after a shampoo."

She stepped forward and picked up a bottle, then reached toward another shelf and selected something else. She had to stand on the tips of her sandaled feet to reach it.

She held both bottles out to Ragnar. "Use as little shampoo as possible, and plenty of this conditioner. Actually, you could even skip the shampoo every other wash and just use this. It'll help with..." she trailed off and gestured at Sophie's head. "You want to work with the curls and not against them." The woman shook her head and smiled. "I'm sorry, I didn't intend to give you a lecture."

Ragnar smiled back. "Don't apologize. I really appreciate the help. Thank you!" He looked at Sophie and saw that the two little girls were eyeing each other, telegraphing signals and sizing each other up in the way that small children do.

"You're welcome," the woman said, then turned to her daughter. "We need to go, Tiffany. Say bye." Her child waved at Sophie, who smiled back, and the mother and daughter walked out of the aisle.

Ragnar stowed the bottles of shampoo and conditioner into his shopping cart. After a moment's thought, he grabbed a few extra bottles. He couldn't count on running into help next time he was at a loss. "We're done, Sophie. Let's head home."

Chapter Three

ELLA STOOD AT the check-out counter feeling as though every eye in the entire grocery store was on her. She keyed in her pin code for the third time, and yet again the words flashed on the screen: "Card declined."

The check-out assistant said, "I'm sorry. Do you have another payment method?"

Ella shook her head, stuffing her debit card back into her purse. Her only credit card was back at home, frozen in a block of ice in the back of her freezer, to be used only in dire emergencies. She dug into her wallet. Thank God! £20. It wouldn't cover all their shopping, but at least it could get them the basics.

"All I've got is this," she said. "Can I just pick out a few things and leave the rest?"

The next customer in the line sighed loudly and checked his watch with an ostentatious jerk of his arm and accompanying eye rolls.

The checkout assistant looked at the man and said in a sweet, sing-song voice, "You might just want to go to the next checkout. I'll be going off duty after this customer."

The man huffed away, and the assistant slid a "till closed" sign onto the conveyor belt. She turned and smiled at Ella. "Don't worry about it, love. Happens a lot more often than you'd think. Just put what you don't want on the side, and I'll scan your items through again. Take your time."

Ella was almost undone by the assistant's kindness, and she fought back tears of humiliation. The lady chatted with Tiffany while Ella picked out only the most essential items from her shopping cart and put them back onto the conveyor belt.

She couldn't understand why her card was declined. There should have been money in her account. The rent from her tenants was past due and ought to have come through by now. She handed over her £20 and the assistant gave her a few pennies back in change, then winked at Tiffany as they headed toward the exit.

Ella made the ten-minute drive back home, then made a beeline for her computer, leaving her groceries in the hallway. She knew she ought to put the chilled items into the fridge, but first she needed to get to the bottom of why her card had been declined. It was the third of the month, and the rent ought to have hit her bank account yesterday at the latest.

She drummed her fingers on her desk while she waited for the machine to creak to life and load her Internet browser. Tiffany kicked off her shoes and went into the living room, settling onto the sofa with her tablet.

Ella logged into her online bank and checked the balance of her current account. The alarming red text and minus signs showed that her account was in overdraft because her mortgage payment had gone out, but no rent had come in. She checked the time. It was probably too late to call the estate agent who managed the property, but she needed to find out what was going on. This wasn't the first time the tenants were in arrears, but the last time they were late with their rent, they had vowed it wouldn't happen again.

Ella's heart was racing as she forced herself to take slow, deep breaths. It was going to be okay. Just a temporary cash flow problem. No need to panic. She did her best to talk herself out of the anxiety that had been all too familiar during her time with Neil.

His extravagant and impulsive spending meant money had always been a worry. He had done the spending and she the worrying, and she never knew which cards were going to be rejected. After he'd died, settling his affairs had been a nightmare. Debt collectors were still calling to this day from random companies who Neil had dealings with.

She pressed her palms together and continued to breathe slowly, counting the seconds as she inhaled and exhaled. She was fine. God had brought them through so much. He'd always provided for her and Tiffany. The real estate agent would let her know what was going on. In the meantime, they had the essential groceries they needed. Plus, she was expecting a payment from her work as a freelance transcriptionist, too, so they were not going to starve. "It'll be okay," she whispered as she stood up to put the shopping away.

"Hey, Mum, it's that girl from Tesco," Tiffany said, peering out of the front window.

Ella paused en route to the kitchen. "Which girl?"

"The one we just saw who was at Tesco with her dad and her rabbit," Tiffany said, pointing.

Ella walked over to the living room window and looked out, blinking in surprise. She recognized the man from the grocery store standing in front of the house opposite hers on the other side of the cul-de-sac. He had one hand on the front door handle while the other pressed a phone to his ear. The little girl stood on the garden path, still holding her furless rabbit, legs crossed in a stance familiar to all parents of small children.

"She looks like she needs a wee," Tiffany said, echoing Ella's thoughts.

The man raised one hand and let it drop sharply to his side, as though in frustration. He looked around, then spoke to the girl, pointing toward a large bush next to the house.

Ella moved away from the window and was out of the front door in seconds. She called out across the road to the man. "Is everything okay?"

He looked up, eyes widening as he saw her. "Oh, hello! Yes. Well, no, I seem to have locked us out and my daughter is desperate for the toilet."

"She's welcome to use ours," Ella said, pointing over her shoulder. "I live just over there."

"Really? Thank you so much!" His face relaxed into a smile. "Sophie, you can have a wee in this lady's house."

The child trotted after Ella, her father following. Ella pushed her front door open and pointed to the bathroom door just off to the left. "In there," she said. She remained on the doorstep while the man stood a few feet away.

"Thank you so much," he said. "I feel like an idiot. I must have locked the keys inside when we went to do our shopping, and of course the spare set is in there, too. I've just been on the phone to the locksmiths, and they say they'll send someone within an hour."

He smiled at her and held out his hand. "I'm Ragnar, by the way. Sophie's my daughter."

"Ragnar," Ella repeated. "That's an unusual name."

"My great-grandfather was from Norway," he said. "It's been a family tradition to give all the children names from the old country. You seem to be our knight in shining armor today. You've rescued us twice already." His brow furrowed. "Knight? Knightess? Lady?"

Ella laughed. "No armor here. Just the right place at the right time, I guess. I'm Ella. I didn't know anyone lived there; it's been vacant since we moved here."

"We've been traveling on an extended trip for a while," Ragnar said. "We just got back last night."

Ella heard movement behind her, and she turned around to see Sophie coming out of the bathroom.

Tiffany had come up, and the girls were examining Sophie's rabbit.

Tiffany looked up at her mother, her face glowing. "Has she come to play with me?"

Ella hesitated, unsure what to say. She glanced at Ragnar, but before he could say anything, his daughter poked her face out of the doorway. "Can I play for a while, please, Dad?"

"Um... we don't know whether Ella and her little girl have plans, sweetheart."

Ella said, "No, we just got in. She's welcome to play for a bit." Thinking he might be hesitant to let his daughter visit with a complete stranger, she added, "Would you like to come in and have a cup of tea while you wait for the locksmith?"

Ragnar smiled. "Thank you! But only if it's no trouble, of course."

"Not at all. Come in," Ella said, stepping back to let him inside.

"Yay!" Tiffany squealed. "Come with me. Clump can meet Ted."

"Is Ted your teddy?" Sophie asked as she followed Tiffany into the living room.

"No. Ted's my elephant," Tiffany said, and the girls continued to chatter away.

Ragnar stepped around the grocery bags, which were still in the hallway. Ella said, "Sorry, I haven't put our things away yet." She looked up at him. "Oh, and if you've just come from Tesco, have you got any groceries you need to keep cold? I mean, until the locksmith lets you in?"

Ragnar raised his hand to his forehead. "Yes, I'd forgotten! I've got some Popsicles that'll soon melt."

"Bring them over and I'll pop them into the freezer," Ella said.

Ragnar went out again, and Ella busied herself with clearing the bags out of the hallway and stowing her groceries away. Ragnar rapped on the open door and came back in holding a plastic bag. He reached in and pulled out a box of fruit Popsicles. "Maybe the girls could share?"

"Those are Tiffany's favorite," Ella said. "Thank you; I'm sure she'd be delighted to have one."

Ella heard the girls' exclamations of delight as Ragnar walked up to them with his box of Popsicles.

"I love those!" Tiffany said. "I wanted some today, but Mum had to give them back to the shop lady because her card was ajeck... ejeck... dejected."

Ella felt her face burning, and she called out to Ragnar to prevent him hearing any further revelations. "Coffee or tea? I've got nothing fancy. Just regular builder's tea and instant coffee."

"Builder's tea is fine." Ragnar walked up to the kitchen counter. "Milk, no sugar, please."

The kettle whistled while Ella set a plate of chocolate digestive biscuits on the kitchen counter. She made the tea and slid Ragnar's mug over. "There you go." She indicated a tall bar stool next to the counter.

Ragnar picked up his mug and a biscuit. "Thanks. I can't resist a chocolate digestive." He took a sip and looked around the living room. "So, how long have you guys been here?"

"We moved here just over a year ago," Ella said. "My mother-in-law Jocelyn owns the main house and we stay here in the granny annex."

"I think I know her by sight if not by name," Ragnar said. "Drives a yellow Volkswagen Beetle?"

"Yes, she used to have one. She traded it in several months ago." She sipped her tea. "So, you said you've been traveling for a while. Been anywhere nice?"

Ragnar smiled. "Yes, we have. We started off in Norway, where I've got some cousins and great aunts. Then we went to Africa so Sophie could spend some time with her grandparents and get to know some of her extended family. And then we stayed a few months in Australia and New Zealand."

"Wow. That was a huge trip," Ella said. Lucky for those who can afford to take a whole year off and travel the world, she thought. She wondered what Ragnar did for a living.

"Yes, it was nice to get away," he said. "But it was time to get back home. I didn't want Sophie to fall too far behind in school. What class is Tiffany in?"

"She would have been going into Year One this autumn, but we're home educating."

Ragnar's eyes widened. "Really? That's interesting." He looked down at his cup of tea and said in a quieter tone, "My wife was interested in home education."

"Did she teach Sophie while you were on your travels?" Ella asked.

Ragnar shook his head. "No. She passed away almost two years ago. It was just Sophie and I who went on that trip."

Ella felt a tug in her heart. "I'm really sorry for your loss. I lost my husband almost two years ago."

Ragnar's glance met hers, and she caught a flash of something in the depth of his gray eyes, a sadness that she recognized all too well. They belonged to a club that nobody wanted to be part of. "I'm sorry for your loss as well," he said.

She couldn't think of anything to say. Thankfully, the girls' chatter filled the silence. Sophie and Tiffany were deep into their game, and

Clump appeared to be hosting a tea party for Ted the elephant and the other toys.

Ragnar pulled his phone out of his pocket in response to a loud beep. He glanced at the screen. "It's the locksmith; he's five minutes away. I'll just wait outside for him. Thank you so much for the tea." He turned to his daughter. "Sophie, it's time to go. Say your goodbyes."

"Aw, Dad, already?" Sophie said. But Ella noticed that she stood up immediately, despite the grumbling.

"Yes, sweetheart," Ragnar said. "Lovely to meet you, Tiffany."

"Nice to meet you too," Tiffany said. "Can she come to play again, Mum?"

Ella glanced at Ragnar. "She can if her dad says it's okay."

"Please, Dad?" Sophie turned her brown eyes to her father, and he ruffled her curls.

"Of course. We'll work something out. But let's get going before we miss the locksmith."

"Bye, Tiffany. Bye, Tiffany's mum," Sophie said.

Ella laughed. "I'm Ella. See you soon. It was lovely having you."

As soon as the clock hit a decent hour the next morning, Ella was on the phone to her estate agent to find out why there was no rental payment in her account. After the second ring, she recognized Charles Appleton's plummy tones.

"Good morning, Mrs. Belmont. How are you?"

"Fine, thanks," Ella said. "Sorry to bother you so early, but there appears to be a delay with my rental payment. It's been a few days since it was due."

"Really? I'm sorry to hear that. I'd hoped that things would get onto an even keel after the talk I had with the tenants."

Ella said, "It did for a while. They paid on time last month, but now they're late again."

"Thanks for letting me know," Charles said. "I'll get in touch with them and find out what's happening and get back to you as soon as I can."

"Thanks. Bye," Ella said. She was glad she didn't have to deal directly with her tenants. She hated having to ask for money, even when it was due to her, and was more than willing to let Charles take a cut of her payment for doing that part of the job for her.

When she'd decided to rent out her family home, Charles Appleton had been thrilled to include her property on his books. He'd been certain that people would be lining up to rent the four-bed house in an affluent village just a half hour's train journey from London. He'd been right, and the property had been snapped up by a young professional couple. But halfway into their twelve-month contract, the tenants had begun to pay their rent later and later, and finally missed a month altogether. Charles had had a talk with them, after which they'd paid more or less on time, but now the money was late again.

Ella had once had the naive view that being a landlord would be like owning a money tree, but she was seeing that this was definitely not the case. What if the payment never came through? She didn't want to fall behind on the mortgage or have to use her credit card to pay it off like the last time this had happened. She was going to have to pick up more hours doing audio transcription work. Perhaps squeeze in another hour of typing before she went to bed and get up an hour earlier. She turned toward her computer to check whether the audio typing agency had posted any work on the job board that she could do tonight.

As she walked past the window, she looked out at the house across the road, and her mind went to the new-to-her neighbors she'd met yesterday. That Sophie was such a sweet little girl, and she'd gotten along so well with Tiffany. Tiffany didn't have many close friends nearby, especially since they'd moved away from Reigate.

That was another casualty in the wake of Neil's death. Most of Tiffany's friends were the children of the couples she and Neil used to hang out with. Young chic couples flying up the career and property ladders, privately schooled professionals who worked hard, played hard, and spent hard. After Neil died and his financial house of cards crumbled so spectacularly, she hadn't seen much of those friends anymore. Perhaps her presence reminded them of their mortality, and her new life living on her mother-in-law's charity made some of them uncomfortable.

She'd been surprised at how little she missed them. She was sorry, though, that Tiffany had lost her playmates. Having Sophie living across the road might turn out to be a real blessing. Her thoughts strayed to Sophie's father. That was an odd coincidence, running into each other like that. Well, perhaps not so odd, considering the size of Hatbrook. Everyone for miles around got their groceries from Tesco.

Ella's mind drifted to comparing Ragnar's dark hair and gray eyes to Neil's pale blond looks, and his lean toned body to Neil's carefully nurtured rugby player's physique. Side by side, there was no question that Neil was the one who would have set more hearts aflutter and turned more heads. He'd certainly addled hers. She'd been so distracted by his physical perfection that she'd ignored a forest of red flags that would have been hard to miss with a less gorgeous man.

That had been one of the many painful lessons she'd learned from being with Neil. She swore that on the remote chance that she was ever looking for a partner again, she would definitely dig beyond the level of their looks, even if they had Ragnar's sea gray eyes.

Chapter Four

RAGNAR SMILED AS he walked behind his daughter. Her excitement was infectious as she rode her scooter down the path toward Hatbrook Common. Even though she hadn't been there in over a year, Sophie clearly still remembered the way. Zuri had brought her here almost every day, and Sophie loved the large green field with the playground tucked at one corner.

It was Saturday afternoon, so there were quite a few children scrambling around the play apparatus. Sophie turned to him and shouted, "Dad, it's Tiffany!" She turned again and made a beeline for the playground, where Ragnar saw the little girl from yesterday hurtling around in circles, pigtails streaming behind her and mouth open in delight while her mother spun her on the merry-go-round.

Ella was laughing as well, and Ragnar's heart squeezed as his mind flashed to a memory of Zuri pushing her squealing child on the same merry-go-round. Zuri had worn her hair in box braids and favored long skirts rather than the faded jeans Ella was wearing, but something about his new neighbor's posture, petite slender figure, and laugh made him think of Zuri.

He raised his hand in greeting, and Ella slowed the merry-go-round down so an eager Sophie could climb on. "We need to stop meeting like this," he said.

She smiled. "I know! I turn around everywhere I go and there you are. Someone would think we lived on the same street." Ragnar laughed, and she reached into her pocket. "Oh! Before I forget. I hope you don't think it's cheeky of me, but I wrote down a couple of YouTube channels by mums with curly-haired mixed-race children. I was planning on popping it through your letter box. Tiffany's hair isn't completely African like mine, so I've had to learn from these videos about how to manage it and what products to use."

Ragnar took the slip of paper she handed to him. "Thanks. YouTube, eh? Why didn't I think of that?"

"There's a lot of good stuff on there," she said.

"I really appreciate it." He tucked the paper into his pocket. Ella began to push the merry-go-round and he joined in to help spin their daughters around. "This is a great park, isn't it?"

"It's lovely," Ella said. "We're out here almost every day in the warm weather. Sometimes we pack a picnic and a bunch of books and just have our lessons out here. And since we home educate, we usually have the whole place to ourselves during school hours."

"That sounds great. Sophie has her first day back at school on Monday," Ragnar said.

"Which school?"

"Just the local village school down the road," Ragnar said. "Hatbrook Primary."

"Oh, nice," Ella said. She addressed her words to Sophie. "Are you looking forward to going?"

Sophie shrugged. "I guess. I hope they let me take Clump. Do you go to that school too, Tiffany?"

Tiffany shook her head. "No, I'm homicated."

"What's homicated?" Sophie asked.

Ragnar could tell Ella was suppressing a laugh, but she managed to keep all but a slight tremor out of her voice. "Home educated means that Tiffany learns at home. I'm her teacher."

"Oh," Sophie said.

"Let's go on the swings!" Tiffany shouted, and the girls ran across the asphalted ground.

"Is home education hard?" Ragnar asked. "I've always admired people who do it."

"It's as hard and as easy as parenting," Ella said. "At her age, we just carry on with what we've been doing since she was a toddler. I read to her, we take lots of nature walks, keep a nature diary, do workbooks for math. I keep an eye on the national curriculum and make sure we're keeping up."

"What about the socialization aspect?" Ragnar asked. "That's what my wife was most concerned about."

Ella smiled. "That's what everyone asks us. Tiffany gets the chance to chat to all sorts of people we meet when we're out and about. We see children her age as well, of course. She goes to Sunday School at church and we have a swimming class and a group that meets to do gymnastics."

"You said you go to church. Which one?" Ragnar asked. She started saying the name and he joined in, chuckling as they completed it together. "Immanuel Hatbrook. Why am I not surprised? I leave the village for a while, then come back and find you guys have taken over all of our regular haunts."

Ella laughed. "Yes, we've been going there since we moved here.

Tiffany absolutely loves it and I do as well. So, you're members there, too?"

"Yes, since we moved to Hatbrook," Ragnar said. "Maybe we'll see you there tomorrow?"

"You probably will, all being well. Hopefully you won't find us sitting in your favorite pew."

Ragnar grinned. "The way things are going, I wouldn't be surprised. Sophie and I had better get there early enough to secure our spots."

They continued chatting, and Ragnar found himself telling her about his work. "I have a software development company. Or, rather, I should say 'had'. I'm in the process of being taken over."

He smiled at the alarm in her face. "It's an entirely voluntary takeover. My partners did a great job holding down the fort when I took an extended leave of absence, and it's time for me to move on.

They've found somebody who wants to buy my share of the company, so now that I'm back, we'll begin sorting out all the details."

"So, a new start for everyone," she said.

Ragnar smiled at her. Yes, indeed. A new start.

As Ella and Tiffany slipped into their seats just before the worship service the next morning, Ella spotted Ragnar and Sophie standing at the back of the sanctuary, surrounded by a knot of eager church members. Sophie held tightly to her father's hand and to her furless rabbit, and Ragnar's smile was broad while he chatted to the little group.

Immanuel Hatbrook felt like home to Ella. She'd gone to church regularly when she'd been younger, but during the years of her marriage to Neil, her attendance had been spotty. Neil had never stopped her from going, and he used to come along with her sometimes, but most Sunday mornings he'd preferred to have a lie-in after a heavy night of partying the night before. When Tiffany was born, Ella wanted her to grow up attending church just like she had, but it had been challenging to fall into a routine.

Since moving to Hatbrook and finding Immanuel, Ella had rarely missed a service. The people at Immanuel were warm and welcoming at more than a surface level, and she enjoyed Pastor Jonathan's sermons. They were full of meat and didn't shy away from or gloss over the very real problems people faced.

Tiffany was thriving in her Sunday School class, and Ella got a lot out of the adults' class, where they regularly dug into the Bible and wrestled with the deeper questions of faith.

And she'd met her closest friend here: Macey Travis. The first hymn began, and Ella smiled as Macey took the seat next to her. They side-hugged, and Ella turned her concentration to the service.

When it was over, they stayed chatting in their seats, and Ella filled Macey in on the latest with her tenants. Macey shook her head so vigorously that her chin-length brown curls jiggled. "That is absolutely crazy. I would have evicted them the very first time they started with those shenanigans. You're far too sweet, Ella. You let everyone walk all over you."

Ella smiled. Despite her hardline talk, Macey was one of the most big-hearted people she knew. "This is coming from the childless and single person who dropped her neighbor's kids off at school for two full terms because their mother couldn't be bothered to get up in the morning?"

Macey grinned. "Touché. But I did it for the little boys. And their mother straightened out her act eventually."

Ella sensed someone standing behind them, and she turned around to see Ragnar and Sophie. She smiled. "Hi! I hope we weren't in your seats."

He laughed. "No. Good to see you here. Hi, Macey. It's been ages."

Ella turned to her friend, then froze when she saw Macey's face. Her beautiful features had hardened, and her lips were compressed in a straight line. As Ella watched, Macey nodded once at Ragnar, then turned her attention to Sophie, her stony expression melting into a warm smile. "Hi, sweetheart. You've become so big!" She engaged the child in small talk while Ella chatted with Ragnar.

Macey stood and looked at Ella. "I've got to go. Catch up with you soon." Without saying a word to Ragnar, Macey turned and headed for the church doors. Ella stared at her friend, puzzled at her curtness. What was that about? Ragnar didn't seem to be fazed, though, so she pushed it out of her mind and turned her attention back to Tiffany, who was pulling her hand to leave.

Chapter Five

A COUPLE OF weeks later, Ragnar stood in front of his daughter, hand churning in his hair, at a complete loss over what to do. Sophie, dressed in her school uniform, slumped in a cross-legged heap on the kitchen floor, tears streaming down her face.

"Sweetheart, we've talked about this," he said. "We need to leave now so you can go to school."

She struggled to get the words out through her sobs. They were the same words she'd been repeating since this tear-filled stand-off began thirty minutes ago. "I... don't... want... to... go!"

He sighed and dropped to his knees so his face could be closer to her eye level. "But I thought it had been going well. Haven't you been making some friends? Learning lots of new things?"

Sophie's only response was to lower her head and cry even more.

He tried again. "Listen, sweetie. It's Thursday. Why don't you go today, and then there'll only be Friday, and we'll have the weekend coming up and we'll get lots of time to do some fun things together. Let's get your shoes on now."

Sophie's tears continued unabated. He wondered where things had all gone wrong. She had been going to the village school for two weeks. She had never been wildly excited about going, but as the days had gone by, what little enthusiasm she had had ebbed away, and it had been getting harder and harder to get her out of the door in the morning. She would drag her feet and ask how many days were left until Friday, wearing a hangdog expression as they made the short walk to the school gates. But today she'd had a complete meltdown.

And of course it had to happen when he had a must-not-miss-unless-you're-on-your-deathbed meeting with the people who were going to buy his stake in Theta Software. His partners badly wanted this deal to go through and he didn't want to let them down. Time was flying by relentlessly and he needed to be at the train station in twenty minutes so he could catch the last possible train that would get him to the meeting on time.

He stood with a sigh. There was no way he could drop Sophie off at school in this state. He didn't know how to handle her when she was like this. Zuri would have known exactly what to do. Was Sophie just being stubborn and needing a firm hand? Or was there something deeper here? She'd been through so much over the last couple of years, more than any five-year-old should. He thought that the daily routine of school would be a good structure to anchor her back into some semblance of normalcy.

Guilt wrenched him inside. Perhaps this huge ramble around the world trip of theirs had done Sophie more harm than good, further destabilizing a life that had been upended with the loss of her mother.

He had convinced himself that it would be good for her, but maybe it was all about him and his need to escape the daily reminders of his life with Zuri. A life that was never coming back. Maybe dragging Sophie along with him had been a terrible idea, when what she'd needed all along had been to settle back into as normal of a life as possible.

Ragnar sighed, mentally chalking up yet another item on the long list of areas where he was failing as a parent. Sophie's face was swollen with crying, her nose and eyes red. He knew that his brother Magnus would step in to take care of Sophie if he'd asked in advance, but there was just no time now. He'd just have to bring her to London and ask Magnus whether he could meet them there and perhaps take Sophie to his office and keep her entertained until Ragnar was done.

Sophie had her shoes on now and was pushing her arms into her jacket. He stroked her hair and kissed her forehead. "Good girl. Let's go."

He double-checked his pockets to make sure he had his house keys before stepping outside. As he stood on the front doorstep, he saw Ella outside her apartment, holding a flowerpot. Tiffany was next to her mother, pink gardening gloves on her small hands, clutching the smallest trowel Ragnar had ever seen.

Tiffany shouted, "Hi, Sophie! Hi, Ragnar."

Ragnar waved back. "Hi. We've got to rush and catch a train to London."

"No school today?" Ella asked.

Ragnar glanced at his daughter. "No, not today."

Ella looked from Ragnar to Sophie, and then scanned his face again. "Doctor's appointment?"

"No. We're just not up to going to school today." He turned to his daughter. "Hurry up, sweetheart. Dad's got a meeting to get to."

He had taken a couple of strides down the road when he heard Ella call out, "We've got a pretty open day today. Sophie is welcome to stay with us if you need to be somewhere."

Ragnar spun around. "What?" Relief washed over him. "Are you sure? It's incredibly kind of you to offer, but I'd hate to impose."

"It's no trouble at all. We'd love to have her."

"Thank you so much!" Ragnar said. "I'm in a crazy rush, but I'm beyond grateful. Sophie, do you hear that? You can stay with Ella and Tiffany today, and we'll talk more about this when I get back home this afternoon."

Sophie's face was alight. It was clear that this change of plans more than met her approval. Ragnar bent over and kissed her forehead.

"All right, sweetheart, off you go, then." He looked up at Ella as Sophie scooted across the yard toward Tiffany. "Thank you. I'll be back between four and five."

"Take your time; we'll be fine. Any food allergies or anything like that we need to know about?"

"No, none. Thanks so much." Ragnar felt like he was repeating himself. He watched as the girls disappeared into the house, then he started down the road. If he walked quickly, he should just about catch the next train.

Compared to the way his morning had begun, Ragnar was surprised at how smoothly his meeting went. The talks with his partners and their lawyers and the prospective buyers and their solicitors were more than cordial, and each party was happy with the terms of how Ragnar was going to relinquish his interests in Theta Software. There would just be an intense transition period over the next three months, but after that his obligations would be over and he'd have a clean slate to start afresh.

He was glad the day of meetings was over. Now, he just needed to deal with this issue of Sophie and school. After he'd called Hatbrook Primary to let them know that she wouldn't be in, he received an email asking him whether he could stop by for a meeting with the head teacher and Sophie's class teacher that afternoon.

He walked into the school building now, along the corridors whose walls were plastered with encouraging slogans in garish colors and row after row of displays celebrating achievements of various sorts. Reading excellence, sporting prowess, care for the environment. He hoped that the head teacher would have some ideas about how to help Sophie settle in.

The hallways were eerily silent, but the school secretary was at her desk and was clearly expecting him. She ushered Ragnar straight into the head teacher's office. He recognized Mrs. Braithwaite from their meeting on Sophie's first day at school. She wore her black hair in a sharply angled bob whose precision matched her tailored dark suit. Her handshake was firm as she greeted Ragnar. He shook hands with the other woman in the room, Sophie's class teacher, Ms. James. She was much younger, probably in her mid-twenties, Ragnar guessed.

"We're so glad you could make it on such short notice, Mr. Klassen," Mrs. Braithwaite said as they settled into their seats. "How is Sophie?"

"She sounded fine when I spoke to her on the phone," Ragnar said. "She's been spending the day with a neighbor."

"I'm glad to hear that," Mrs. Braithwaite said. She had a file open in front of her and glanced at it before continuing. "It's an odd coincidence that Sophie had that episode this particular morning. We were planning on calling you in for a conference soon to discuss how your daughter is settling in school, and her refusal to come in today has escalated matters."

Ragnar felt a knot begin to form in his stomach. "Okay," he said, looking back and forth at the two women.

"Yes," Mrs. Braithwaite said. "Mr. Klassen, from your perspective, how do you think Sophie is getting on at school?"

Ragnar said, "She seems to be taking a lot longer than I had hoped to find her groove. She was never very keen about starting school, but as time has gone by, she's lost whatever little enthusiasm she had. She

laughs. When we went on our trip abroad, she seemed to really blossom, meeting new people and getting to know her extended family. I didn't see any signs of anxiety or distress until we came back and started trying to get into a school routine."

Mrs. Braithwaite and Ms. James exchanged looks. The head teacher said, "Our only experience with Sophie is what we've observed here, and that is enough to cause significant concern. We would strongly recommend that you try to access some sort of bereavement service. As a school, we're only just developing our own bereavement policy, something which we are aware should ideally have been in place before now. But there are some very good organizations and resources that we can recommend." She picked up a handful of brochures and passed them on to Ragnar.

He took them mechanically. "Thanks. I can look at these and see what else we can do at home. I appreciate that you're working to get a... what did you call it? A bereavement policy in place, and it's great that you'll be better able to help children in the future. But what are you doing right now? How are you going to support my daughter tomorrow if she comes in? From what you say, she's having a miserable time here even though she's okay everywhere else."

Ms. James said, "We'll continue to do what we can, of course. But it's important that she gets the professional help she needs so that she can cope with the school setting and learn."

Ragnar held up one hand. "Forgive me if I'm not understanding this. Did you say the purpose of this professional therapy would be to help her settle into school?"

The women looked at each other again, and Ms. James said, "Yes. That would be an important part of it."

Ragnar closed his eyes. He thought of the moment he had first held Sophie. He'd stared into her scrunched-up face with its cap of dark hair, already thick even then. She was from his own body, part of his own blood. She was completely helpless. And she needed him.

While stroking her tiny cheek and marveling at how perfect she was, he had known a visceral, primal urge to protect her, to keep her safe from anything that threatened her. To crush and obliterate anything that caused her harm or fear. The same feeling rose up now, making it hard to keep his voice steady and his thoughts rational.

He spoke slowly. "I'm trying to get my head around all this. I'm not opposed to the idea of therapy, but what I don't understand is why should a five-year-old who's lost her mother have to conform for the sake of this school? Shouldn't you have enough flexibility to accommodate a child of her age, given all she's been through?"

He caught the look the women exchanged, and he held up his hand. "I'm sorry. I know I'm sounding combative. And I know that you are professionals and have a lot more experience than I do handling children in general, even those who have trouble settling in school."

He looked at each of them in turn. "But I am Sophie's father. I've seen my child not merely coping after we lost her mother but flourishing and growing. Until she came here. Please don't get me wrong. I'm not saying that this school is a bad place; it's clearly wonderful for most of the other children. But maybe it just isn't the best place for Sophie right now. She's doing wonderfully everywhere else, but maybe she just isn't robust enough to deal with the particular challenges that this school setting presents. And if that's the case, I wonder whether it isn't more harmful to keep her here while she's still growing and healing."

"What are you saying, Mr. Klassen?" Mrs. Braithwaite asked.

"I'm saying that based on the complete meltdown I saw today, and what you're telling me about what an awful time she's having here, maybe it would be best to withdraw her for the time being and re-enroll her in a few months when she's a bit more mature."

Ms. James said, "I'm not sure whether I would advise that. The daily routine and schedule could be an important anchor for her during this time."

"Maybe," Ragnar said. "I admit that's what I hoped. But I've rarely seen her as upset as she was when I was trying to get her in to school this morning. I just can't reconcile in my mind that this is what she needs right now, being forced to go to a place where you yourselves admit she's been anxious and weepy enough to worry you. How can that help?"

"Well, it's not entirely unusual for children to experience separation anxiety when they've just started school," Ms. James said.

"I understand that," Ragnar said. "But have those children also lost their mother in a hit and run?"

Ms. James looked at her hands and didn't answer.

Mrs. Braithwaite said, "She will need to learn to cope with a school setting eventually. It's important that she learns to face challenging situations instead of being shielded from everything. She'll need to learn resilience."

"You don't teach a non-swimmer resilience by throwing them into a shark-infested sea with no life jacket," Ragnar snapped. Ms. James winced, and Mrs. Braithwaite started. Ragnar was shocked by the sharpness of his own tone.

He held up his hands. "I'm sorry; I didn't mean to raise my voice. I appreciate all you've done, and I guess you've done the best you can, given some really tough and unusual circumstances. And, like I said, I'm glad that you're putting a bereavement policy in place, and I understand how that will help your pupils. It may be selfish of me, but I'm not thinking about other people's children in the future. I'm thinking about my daughter right now, and I've made up my mind.

Please let me have whatever paperwork I need to withdraw her from the school."

Chapter Six

THE REPERCUSSIONS OF what he'd just done began to sink in as Ragnar left the head teacher's office and began the short walk back home. He'd never had a problem making decisions. Zuri had always said he tended to decide first and rationalize later. Had he just done that?

He and Sophie were supposed to be getting their lives back on track, piecing together some form of normalcy. The plan was supposed to be to give his daughter a stable childhood and raise her into a well-adjusted human being. It was bad enough that he'd taken her along in his wanderings across three continents when all her age-mates were settling into kindergarten and Year One. And now, by yanking her out of school, hadn't he just torpedoed her chances of a settled childhood?

And just where was she supposed to hang out now that she wasn't in school? He still had several weeks of intense work ahead to complete his company handover. Maybe he'd been too hasty taking her out before he'd put some other arrangements in place. But he remembered Sophie's tears, her broken sobs begging him not to make her go in, and he knew there wasn't anything else he could have done.

Legally, Sophie didn't need to be in full-time education until this September. That would give her a few more months of breathing space.

Maybe she'd be ready to start school by then.

He came up to Ella's front door and rang the bell. Thank God she'd been able to take care of Sophie today.

Ella opened the door and met him with a smile. A delicious aroma wafted out, reminding him of how long it had been since the sandwich he'd snatched at noon. Her stripy apron was dusted with flour, which also covered her hands. "Hi, Ragnar. Come in. Sophie, your dad's here," she called over her shoulder, then stepped back so Ragnar could walk into the hallway.

Sophie came running up to him, coated with even more flour than Ella. She was grinning from ear to ear, fizzing with excitement. "Hi, Dad! We've been baking cookies. Ella let me use her mixer. And now we're putting icing on them. Come and see, Dad!"

He followed his daughter to the kitchen counter, where Tiffany was sitting on a bar stool. Sophie climbed onto the second stool and pushed over to Ragnar a star-shaped sugar cookie buried under purple icing, sprinkles, and Smarties.

"That looks amazing, sweetheart," Ragnar said.

"You can eat that one, Dad. I'm just going to start another one. I'll put pink icing on this one."

As Ragnar looked at his daughter, absorbed in decorating her cookie, her new friend leaning over and handing her the pink sprinkles, his mind went back to the class teacher's words. "Anxious and withdrawn." He smiled and stroked her hair.

Ragnar turned around to face Ella. "Thank you so much for taking care of her today. Was she okay?"

"We had a blast." Ella gestured to the girls. "It's been like this pretty much all day. I don't know which one of them has enjoyed herself more."

"That's great," Ragnar said. "Do you have a moment? I was in such a rush to get out this morning that I didn't get a chance to explain what this is all about."

They walked to the other side of the living room, and Ragnar lowered his voice after checking that the girls' full attention was on their cookie decorating. "School hasn't been going well for Sophie. This morning she absolutely refused to go in, which is why I was so glad that you were able to watch her. I've just been in a meeting with the school head and Sophie's class teacher, and it seems she's getting on even worse than I thought. Anyway, I've just pulled her out with immediate effect."

"I'm really sorry to hear it's not worked out," Ella said.

"Me too. I felt it just wasn't the right environment for her. But it means that I've got to get some sort of childcare in place. It's really cheeky of me to ask, but could you watch her for me tomorrow? I really understand if you can't. I should be able to work something out with my brother. I'll—"

"Done." Ella said. "Just drop her here when you're on your way out."

Ragnar stared at her, slack-jawed, stunned at how quickly she'd agreed. "Thank you!" he stammered.

Chapter Seven

ELLA FELT HER phone buzzing in her pocket the next afternoon as she watched Sophie and Tiffany playing together on Hatbrook Common. She pulled her phone out and glanced at the display. It was Charles Appleton, her estate agent, returning a call she'd made that morning.

"Hi, Charles. I hope you've got something good to tell me. You said that the tenants were supposed to send me weekly payments to make up for the missed rent. Well, I got something a couple of days after you spoke with them, but since then there's been nothing. They're still several hundred pounds short."

"That's why I'm calling, Mrs. Belmont," he said. "I have a bit of news regarding your tenants. I've attempted to contact them several times over the past few days, but they haven't engaged with me. Given their continued withholding of rent and their persistent lack of communication, I would advise you to begin eviction proceedings."

"Wow, okay," she said. "Are you sure? You've tried going to the house? I mean, I'm sure you've done everything properly, but—"

"Yes, I've followed our standard procedure at every point. I've sent a letter by registered post, I've attempted to call them on the numbers they left on record, and I've been by the house. I'm certain that somebody was present, but they didn't answer the door. I'm sorry it's come to this, but they are in breach of contract and have left us with no other choice."

"What will happen now if we go ahead and do this?" Ella asked.

"We'll file a Section 8 notice, on the grounds of non-payment and repeated rent arrears. Following that, I'll apply to the court for a possession order."

"How much notice will they get?" Ella asked.

"We can ask for them to get between two weeks and two months," Charles said. "It's up to you."

Ella was silent for a moment. She wanted to be reasonable and give them time to find somewhere else. But at the same time, she was counting on the money the house was supposed to be bringing in. If the process dragged on too long, she was going to be in a financial hole. "Let them have one month's notice," she said.

"Are you sure?" Charles said. "Your insurance will cover missed or delayed rental payments, but if we lodge a claim, it may take some weeks before they pay out."

Ella sighed. "Give them a month and go ahead with the rest. Do I have to sign anything?"

"My office is open on Saturday, so if you could stop by tomorrow morning, I'll have all the documents you need."

"Thanks," she said, and he ended the call.

She opened her calendar app and did some mental calculations. If it came to the worst and she never saw a penny from these people until they'd left the house, she'd need to figure out how to cover at least the next two mortgage payments until her insurance came through. And how long would it take until she could get new tenants in? The move-in process had happened really quickly when these people took the property. Hopefully, it would go just as fast again.

But finances were going to be tight for a while. Her thoughts slid into a prayer. *Lord, please help me figure something out. You've always made a way for us to stay on top of things. Please provide the money to keep the mortgage paid while this situation with the tenants is sorted out.*

She glanced up at the girls, who were engrossed in a game of hopscotch. As soon as they went back home, she'd see whether the transcription agency had any work available. There was usually no shortage of projects, and her only limitation was the number of hours she was physically available to do the work.

That was another thing to be thankful to God for. When she'd been pregnant with Tiffany, she had started doing online transcription work as a freelance contractor.

It was perfect because she could do it at home and choose her own hours. She'd figured out that if she worked full time outside the home, the cost of childcare would have wiped out most of what she'd be earning. She'd known for a while that she didn't have the sharp elbows and ambition necessary to make it in the cut-throat world of advertising. That was where she'd met Neil, when she was an intern fresh from university and he was a rising star in the firm.

A shout from the girls jolted her out of her thoughts and made her look up. They were laughing as they scrambled up the climbing frame. She smiled as she watched them. Ragnar's daughter was a lovely child, and such great company for Tiffany.

Her transcription job had turned out to be a godsend. Neil earned a generous wage as a marketing executive, and he regularly earned large bonuses on top, but money seemed to fly out the door as soon as it came in. Her little side income gave her a tiny measure of control, and it had been a lifeline after the financial firestorm that followed Neil's death.

She worked while Tiffany was in bed, managing to squeeze in about four hours of typing in the evenings and early morning. She wondered whether she could stretch it up to six hours. She'd have to, if she was going to keep the mortgage paid. At least the weather was warming up. Living costs in spring and summer were always much cheaper than in the colder months.

Once again, she gave thanks for the free accommodation Jocelyn had given her, and the bereavement pension which covered their basic needs. But she hated this constant stress over money. She was going to have to sit down and figure something out.

She glanced at her watch. They'd need to get back home now so they'd be in when Ragnar stopped by to collect Sophie.

The girls were watching *My Little Pony* together at Ella's place when Ragnar arrived.

"Hi, sweetheart. It'll be time to go soon," he said.

"Aw, Dad, can I watch until the end of the episode?" Sophie pleaded.

"Okay. Just this one, though." He accepted Ella's offer of tea and sat at the kitchen counter. "Have they had a good day?"

"Lovely," Ella said. "We did Tiffany's reading and writing work. Sophie joined in, too. Then we went for a nature walk, and they just played the rest of the day. Made lunch, played with play dough, had a teddy bear tea party... it's been great."

Ragnar smiled. "I'm so glad to hear that," he said. He rested his elbows on the counter and steepled his fingers together. "I've been thinking a bit, and I've got a proposal for you. Please don't answer straight away unless it's an immediate no, of course."

Ella turned to look at him, pausing as she stood at the sink with the kettle in her hand.

"Would you consider being Sophie's official child-minder? On a regular and paid basis?" he asked. "I'd give you an hourly rate and we could work out whatever terms you'd like. I know it's out of the blue, but I'd really appreciate it if you'd give it some thought."

Ella's eyes grew wide. "Wow, that is a surprise. It hardly feels like work having her around."

"Maybe not now, but you're doing both of us a great service," he said. "And with an extra child, your costs will be up. If nothing else, I need to compensate you for meals, supplies for whatever crafts you're doing, activities and outings, not to mention your time. And you'd be doing something that I'd otherwise need to pay for anyway. I can't ask you to do it for free. Please think about it."

She smiled. "Okay, I'll think and pray about it."

"Thank you." He held her gaze. "But I really don't want you to feel pressured. If you can't do it, or don't want to do it, just say no. You don't even need to give a reason."

"I appreciate that." She turned away and filled up the kettle.

"When would you need an answer?"

"As soon as possible," he said. "My sister-in-law will take care of Sophie next week, so an answer sometime within the next few days would be ideal."

"Okay, I'll let you know as soon as possible."

"Great! Thank you," Ragnar said. There was a notepad on the counter. He pulled out a pen and wrote down a figure, then turned the paper around. "And just to put it out there and avoid any awkwardness, this is what I'd propose as an hourly wage."

Ella's heart thumped as she looked at the number. It was more than generous. That amount of extra income would go a long way toward plugging in the gaps in her rental income. She hoped her face was neutral as she smiled again at Ragnar.

Chapter Eight

"AND IS THIS new child-minding arrangement permanent now?" Jocelyn asked, handing a glass of juice to Ella. She had invited Ella and Tiffany to make the most of an unseasonably warm spring evening by barbecuing in her backyard. Jocelyn's partner, Jarvis Mullins, had joined them.

Ella supposed he qualified to be called a partner since he and Jocelyn had been in a relationship for over a year. Somewhere in his mid-to-late-fifties, Jarvis worked in the City at some sort of high finance job. He was obviously aware of his ostentatiously good looks and liked to flash his cash as well as his slightly-too-white teeth.

Ella had never warmed to him, but she was glad that he had come on the scene at a time when Jocelyn needed comfort and distraction in the wake of Neil's death. Now, as his eyes roved over her body, lingering on her legs, she wished she'd worn a shapeless dress instead of the knee-length skirt she had on.

She replied to Jocelyn's question. "The first weeks have gone really well, and we're all happy with how Sophie's settled in. So, we'll carry on into and possibly through the summer."

"Is he planning on sending her back to school at some point?" Jocelyn asked, stopping with her tray in front of Jarvis. He took a glass of Pimm's and downed a long sip, smacking his lips with relish.

"I don't think he's planning on enrolling her until the new school year at least," Ella said. "But that's really none of my business."

"And what kind of a child is she? Does she play well with my little Tiffany?"

"She's lovely," Ella said, with a smile. "They get along really well. If anything, Tiffany's the one who likes to take charge, but I think they're really good for each other."

"I'm glad to hear that," Jocelyn said, settling down in her chair.

"I understand this neighbor of yours is one of the Klassen family," Jarvis said. "Related to Karl Klassen." He lifted the hood of the grill and poked at the pork chops with his tongs. Smoke wafted out, bearing a fragrant tang to Ella's nose.

"I don't know his family," she said.

"Yes, I believe he's the eldest son," Jocelyn said. "We were all surprised when he moved into our road. I read about his mother in *Hello* magazine, when the family bought Hambley Heath Manor. There was a two-page spread showing the house."

Jarvis cocked an eyebrow. "Bet he's loaded."

"Yes," Jocelyn said, "although you wouldn't really know it. He doesn't act posh at all. I don't know him much to speak to, but he seems really down to earth. Drives a Vauxhall. They moved here when their child was quite young, and he seemed to work really long hours, so I didn't see that much of him. I used to take in the odd parcel for them. Say hello... that sort of thing. Then his poor wife died before I'd gotten to know them. And then, of course, we were going through our own troubles with poor Neil."

"What sort of work does he do?" Jarvis asked. "In the family business, I suppose."

"Something in software development," Ella said, reluctant to share any information with Jarvis.

"Well, as long as he's paying you fairly for the work you're doing," Jocelyn said. "Oh, I'd better get out the salad." She went off to the kitchen.

Jarvis turned his gaze back to Ella. "It's a nice arrangement for you, to be sure. Wealthy widower entrusts attractive young widow with his child. It's the perfect setup. Perhaps he'll be easily consoled." The leer that twisted his mouth made his face ugly.

Heat rushed up to Ella's face, and anger choked her words. Jarvis only dropped remarks like that when his partner was well out of earshot. She stood up, jostling the side table, and went toward the kitchen to check whether Jocelyn needed any help.

Jocelyn insisted that she had everything well in hand, but Ella hung around the kitchen until it was time to eat. Tiffany had been playing in the living room, and Ella ensured she hadn't gone out to the back yard on her own with Jarvis. She had no idea what that man was capable of saying to her child if she wasn't present, given the inappropriate remarks he delighted in aiming her way.

They all went back outside where Jarvis had laid out the meat onto serving platters. Jocelyn praised him for his qualities as a barbecue chef while Ella ate quietly.

"We have some other exciting news," Jocelyn said, casting a coy glance at Jarvis.

"Oh?" Ella said.

"Jarvis's work is sending him to manage a project in Greece. He'll be there for about three or four months, and he's asked me to go with him!"

"That sounds lovely," Ella said. She forced a civil smile to her lips. "Congratulations, Jarvis."

Jarvis flashed his fluorescent teeth. "Thank you. Maybe you and Tiffany might want to pop on over while we're down there. It'll be gorgeous bikini weather."

Ella's skin crawled, but Jocelyn just giggled. Ella was glad when her phone buzzed, giving her an excuse not to answer Jarvis's comment. It was her estate agent. She hadn't heard from him since she'd signed the papers giving him the go-ahead to start the eviction process.

"I've got to take this. Sorry," she said, and got up from the table, heading to the camellia bushes, which were now in their full spring glory.

"Hello, this is Ella," she said.

"Hello, Mrs. Belmont. I hope I haven't called at a bad time," Charles Appleton said.

"No, not at all. I'm guessing you have news about the tenants?"

"Yes," the agent said. "There's no easy way to tell you this. I have bad news about the house."

Chapter Nine

ELLA COULD HARDLY hear her own voice above her thudding heart. "Bad news?" she repeated.

"Yes," Charles said. "The tenants were served with their Section 8 notice, and we were in the process of getting a possession order when we were informed that the property had been vacated."

"So, they're gone?" Ella asked.

"Yes. An agent who manages a property in the area advised me that it was vacant."

"The tenants didn't tell you themselves?" Ella asked.

"No. They cleared out of the house and left it unsecured. My colleague told me the door was standing open."

Ella couldn't believe what she was hearing. "So, they moved out without telling you and left the house open?"

Charles said, "Yes. I went there immediately, of course, and found that the tenants did indeed appear to have vacated the property. Many of their personal effects are gone, but there is a significant amount of clutter still in place. And I'm afraid they have left the property in extremely poor condition. You'll want to see it yourself, of course, but I recommend hiring an independent evaluator to inspect the damage."

Ella sank into a bench. "Damage? How bad is it?"

Charles cleared his throat. "I'm not qualified to give an estimate.

But I would be shocked if they expect to get their deposit back."

"What do I do? What's the next step?"

"I've taken possession of the property, of course," Charles said. "New locks have been installed. I think it would be advisable for you to go down to the house and see it for yourself, then you can instruct us further when you're clear about what your options are."

"Okay," Ella said. She found Charles' formal language oddly comforting, as though this was all a technical and theoretical matter far removed from her, and not the trashing of her principal source of livelihood. "Would you meet me there?"

"Yes, of course," Charles said. "Would twelve o'clock tomorrow suit you?"

Ella's mind flew to Sophie. She was supposed to be watching her tomorrow. She'd have to tell Ragnar to make alternative arrangements. She hated to let him down at short notice, but she needed to see the house. And maybe Jocelyn could look after Tiffany. It would be in the daytime, so Jarvis would not be around.

"Okay, I'll meet you there tomorrow," Ella said.

Ella knocked at Ragnar's door later that evening. She had his phone number, but she'd rather speak to him face to face. Tiffany was in bed, so she thought it would be okay to step across the road, since her apartment was just a few feet away.

Ragnar opened the door, his face registering surprise when he saw her. His smile was just as immediate. "Hi, Ella. Everything okay?"

"I'm really sorry about the short notice, but something's come up and I can't watch Sophie tomorrow," she said.

"Oh. Okay. I'm sorry to hear that." He peered closer at her. "I hope nothing's wrong."

She read the concern in his eyes and blurted out, "It's my house. Not this one; the one that I've been renting out. The tenants have gone and trashed the place, and I need to meet with the estate agent tomorrow and inspect the damage."

"You absolutely need to take care of that," he said. "Don't worry about Sophie. Is there anything I can do? Do you need me to watch Tiffany for you? I'll arrange to work from home so that Sophie can stay with me. I'm sure she'd love Tiffany's company."

"It's really kind of you to offer that," she said. "My mother-in-law said she would watch Tiffany, but it means she'll have to cancel an appointment she's waited ages for."

Ragnar raised his hands. "I'll do it. More than willingly. If you don't mind leaving her here, that is."

Relief flooded Ella. "Would you? Thank you so much! I can't tell you how much I appreciate that. Can I drop her over at ten? I should be back around three or four."

"That's fine. Good luck. I really am sorry."

"Thank you. Good night, and see you soon, then," she said. She heard his door click shut as she crossed the road and knocked on Jocelyn's door. Jarvis's BMW was still parked outside. She didn't want to interrupt their date, but she'd better tell Jocelyn about the change in arrangements before she canceled her appointment.

Jocelyn stood in her doorway. "Hi, sweetheart. Forget something?"

"No, it's about tomorrow," Ella said. "Thanks so much for stepping in, but I've managed to get somebody else to watch Tiffany, so you don't need to reschedule with the consultant."

Jocelyn's penciled eyebrows flew up. "Oh, right. Thank you. Who's going to watch her?"

Ella gestured with her thumb at Ragnar's house. "Ragnar will."

Jocelyn pursed her lips and said a long, "Oh." Ella wished she would come out with whatever was on her mind, but Jocelyn said, "All right, then. Good luck. Let me know how it goes." She went back into her house and the presumably waiting Jarvis.

Chapter Ten

ELLA WALKED UP the garden path to her former family home. Charles Appleton stood on the front step, looking just like he sounded on the phone: prim, proper, with everything in place. His silver hair was swept back from a smooth unlined forehead, and his perfectly tailored suit draped his slim, tidy figure. Ella felt scruffy in her faded denim skirt and un-ironed cotton shirt, her hair hidden under a colorful wrap. She'd had a restless night, and she knew it showed.

Even as she approached the door, she could see that the tenants had neglected the place at best. Trash lay scattered over the front lawn, and the unkempt grass was fighting a losing battle for space against a virulent crop of weeds. The potted shrubs were withered, and dust lay thick on the windowsill.

Charles stretched out his hand and she took his smooth grip. "Good afternoon, Mrs. Belmont," he said. "I'm very sorry to see you under these circumstances. Shall we go in? Or perhaps you would rather go in yourself first. On such occasions, particularly when this has been your family home, it's been my experience that clients often prefer to view the property in private."

"Thank you," Ella said. Charles remained outside as she stepped through the front door.

She thought that Charles' words would have prepared her for what she would see, but the house looked worse than anything she had imagined. Her breath quickened as her eyes swept over the entryway. The floor was barely visible through the litter and encrusted dirt. Light fixtures were ripped out, a hole had been punched through one wall, and it appeared as though someone had tried to pull the radiator out.

The door leading to the downstairs bathroom had been torn off and hung from one hinge at a crazy angle. The walls were streaked with nameless filth, and she had to step around a pile of junk that blocked the way into the open plan living room.

She walked through to the kitchen, which had been her favorite room in the house. Something sticky on the floor was gumming up her shoes. It was the sight of the

back splash that undid her. She remembered spending ages poring
over tile samples, agonizing over
which ones she should choose to
line the wall behind the sink. The
Roman Silver tiles she'd chosen
with such care were cracked and
coated with grime now, and dirt
blackened the farmhouse sink.

Her eyes filled with tears, and she
turned around and groped her way
to the staircase. She lowered herself
onto one of the steps, numb to
whatever it was that crunched underneath her. She covered her face
with her hands, hulking sobs ripping through her body.

Even as she wept, she knew that
she wasn't just grieving the house.
This had once been her beautiful
home. Her marital home. It lay in
ruin now, not just neglected but de-
liberately destroyed. Like her
marriage. That had been beautiful
once, too. She'd said yes to a heart-

stoppingly handsome man who swept her off her feet with his charm, blowing past her defenses like a force of nature.

The vandalized house around her was the physical manifestation of the wreckage of her all her dreams. As sobs shook her body, she was mourning the marriage she never had, the husband who she had lost twice—first when his love for her faded into bored indifference and he'd sought bigger thrills through substance abuse, gambling, and a possible extramarital affair, and again when he'd died, leaving her to deal with the fallout of his financial mismanagement.

The whole world knew about his death. But nobody could share her bitter tears over her other losses, the ones that cut the deepest, leaving festering wounds that she kept hidden. She wasn't sure whose shame she was trying to cover up—

Neil's or her own. So, she let his mother, her family and friends keep the memory of the public-facing Neil with the irresistible charm. Everyone's favorite guy.

She always smiled bravely when they whispered, "Poor Ella. She must be devastated over losing such a great husband." She never said a word about the Neil who was behind the facade.

Through her tears, Ella was vaguely aware of the front door opening and steps coming across to her. She looked up when a hand touched her shoulder. Charles Appleton stood in front of her, holding out a white handkerchief. Of course Charles would have a perfectly laundered linen handkerchief. Who else even used the things these days? His blue eyes were full of sympathy, and that set Ella's tears off again. She accepted the hankie and blew her nose, then wiped her eyes.

"I'm deeply sorry, Mrs. Belmont," Charles said, looking around. "I completely understand and sympathize with your distress. What they did here is an utter disgrace. The worst I've seen, and I have seen a lot. It is a consolation that the tenants are gone and the house is back in your possession."

His sincerity warmed her frozen and battered heart. She managed a smile. "Thank you. I've seen enough; I don't think I need to go through the rest of the house."

"That's probably best, I agree," he said, offering her his hand as she stood up.

"I know I need to deal with this, but I can't think right now." She rubbed her temples with her fingers. "I just need some time to process all of this before I can even get my head around what to do next."

He nodded his sympathy. "I'll call you and talk you through your options."

Chapter Eleven

THE SECOND RAGNAR saw Ella, he knew something was wrong. She was back to pick up Tiffany after her inspection of her house. She smiled, but Ragnar could tell that it took a lot of effort. He knew what it looked like when every ounce of your strength was channeled into holding up a brave front.

"Come in," he said, closing the door behind her as she walked into his hallway. He watched her as she looked around his living room, taking in the tasteful decor, done in shades that complemented key accents of Zuri's favorite color, robin egg blue.

He motioned toward a sofa, and Ella sat on the edge, fists clenched on her knees. "Was it bad?" he asked.

She nodded, her chin trembling slightly. "I'm glad Tiffany didn't see it."

The girls clattered down the stairs, and Tiffany hurled herself into her mother's arms. "Hi, Mum!"

Ella's face softened as she held her daughter. "Hi, sweetheart! Wow, look at you!"

"We've been playing princesses," Tiffany said, twirling around. She had draped a mismatched collection of silky scarves around her body and wrapped layers of costume jewelry around her neck and wrists. Sophie was dressed equally extravagantly.

"Delighted to meet you, your royal highnesses," Ella said, and Tiffany managed a wobbly curtsy. Sophie tried one as well, tripped, and bumped into Tiffany. Both girls fell into a giggling heap, and Ella laughed.

Sophie got up and tugged on her friend's arm. "Come on," she said, and they charged up the stairs again.

Ella turned back to Ragnar, and his heart warmed up at how her smile eased the tension from her face. "Not hard to see what kind of day they've had," she said. "I hate to drag Tiffany off, but I'd better get her home and sort out something for tea."

"Do you have to?" Ragnar asked. Ella blinked at him and he went on, "I mean, you don't need to rush off. It's been ages since I've seen Sophie have such a great time. It's Friday and I haven't got any plans. Why not make an evening of it? Eat lots of rubbish for dinner, binge watch

Disney movies, and play princesses. And that's just me. I'm sure we can think up something for the girls to do as well."

Ella laughed. "You know what? That's a very tempting idea. But I'm not sure..."

"Go on, you know you want to," Ragnar said.

"Oh, all right," Ella said. "I've got some frozen pizza and popcorn at my place. And between my streaming accounts, I have access to every Disney movie ever made."

"Excellent! I'll bring fizzy drinks."

She stood up. "Okay. Give me a little while to sort myself out and pop the pizzas in the oven. Bring the girls over in about half an hour?"

"Sounds good," he said.

Ragnar couldn't remember whose idea it had been for the girls to have a sleepover, but after back-to-back viewings of *Aladdin*—cartoon and live action—and *Moana*, the girls were tucked up in sleeping bags in Tiffany's room. He didn't know who had had more fun singing along through all the movies. He kept covertly watching Ella throughout the evening and was happy to see how she had relaxed. She came back into the living room, half-closing the bedroom door behind her.

"They're both wiped out," she said.

Tangled was on the screen now, frozen on a frame from the opening sequence. It had been the last movie they'd started before the girls crashed. Ragnar gestured at the TV. "I don't really have an excuse now that the girls are gone, but it's been a while since I watched this one. Mind if we finish it?"

Ella smiled. "No excuse needed." She settled back onto the sofa and handed him a bowl of popcorn. He was sitting on the recliner, legs stretched out. "It's one of my favorites."

He hit the remote and the film continued. He watched for several minutes then said, "Who's the actress who plays Rapunzel, again?" There was no answer, so he glanced at Ella. She lay curled up on the sofa, her eyes closed. Her hand rested over her chest and her breathing was slow and even. She was fast asleep.

"Ella?" he said quietly, but she didn't respond.

He stared at her face, admiring the contours of her cheeks, her nose, her lips, and her flawless skin. He felt guilty for looking at her and turned away. He stood up quietly and picked up one of the velvety blankets the girls had been snuggling in as they watched the movies. He laid it over Ella, pulling it up to her chin. She didn't stir. She must have been exhausted. She had looked close to the edge when she came back this afternoon.

They hadn't had much of a chance to talk about the house, but she'd said enough so he knew she had been shaken by what she saw. He couldn't imagine what that must have felt like. He was grateful that he'd had a chance to see her laugh after going through that and hoped that he'd helped in some small measure. Sleep would do her good. His eyes strayed to her face again. She poured so much of herself into taking care of the girls all day. Who took care of her when her strength ran out?

Ragnar picked up the remote and clicked the TV off. He half-expected her to wake up when the sound of the movie stopped, but she didn't move. He went to the kitchen counter and picked up a notepad and wrote, "Thanks for a lovely evening. Send Sophie over as early as you like. R."

He propped the notepad up in front of the bowl of popcorn on the coffee table, then checked the back door to make sure it was locked.

He crossed over to the front door. It had a deadlatch and should lock itself automatically. He went back to the living room and looked down at Ella again. She still hadn't moved. He found the light switch on the wall and turned the living room lights off. He let himself out of the house, careful to close the door softly, listening for the quiet click of the deadlatch.

As he crossed the road, he saw movement out of the corner of his eye. He looked up in time to see a

curtain twitching in Jocelyn's window.

Chapter Twelve

ELLA SAT UP, bewildered, wondering where she was. A blanket slid off her onto the floor, and she realized she was on her sofa. The house was dark and quiet. Her phone was on the coffee table, and she grabbed it to check the time. 3:22 am.

As she picked it up, she bumped a notepad that had been propped up on a bowl. She looked at the writing on it. "Thanks for a lovely evening. Send Sophie over as early as you like. R." Oh, no. She'd fallen asleep in front of him. Had she snored? Drooled? Or even worse?

She stood up, smoothing out her skirt. How long had she been asleep? It must have been at least five hours. She was used to being tired. Over the last few nights, she had stayed up into the wee hours to get her typing work done. She needed the extra cash, but the late nights were catching up to her. She went to Tiffany's room and eased the door open. The girls were sleeping peacefully.

Ella went to the bathroom and picked up her toothbrush. She had enjoyed herself last night. More than she'd thought possible. Ragnar had been completely right. Chilling out with junk food and Disney movies had been the perfect antidote to the stress and immense well of sadness she'd felt after looking at the house.

She knew that she still needed to deal with all the practicalities of it, but she felt like life was full of more light than she had thought. Instead of curling up into a ball and isolating herself, which was her usual way of dealing with her sorrow, she'd been able to relax, unwind, and laugh. With a friend. That had felt good.

She pulled on a night shirt and crawled into her bed. Teetering again on the brink of slumber, she breathed a prayer. *Lord, thank you for last night. Thanks for my new neighbors. Thank you for the chance to relax and rest with a friend.*

She was straightening up the living room early the next morning when there was a knock on the door. It was probably Ragnar coming to get Sophie. She'd tell him the girls were still asleep. She opened the front door and blinked in surprise. Jocelyn stood on the door-step, hand on one hip.

"Good morning, Ella. Expecting someone else?"

"Hi, Jocelyn. I thought that it might be Ragnar coming to pick up his daughter. She had a sleepover with Tiffany last night."

"Ah, it was only the girls who had a sleepover," Jocelyn said. Her tone set Ella on edge.

"Yes," she said, keeping her voice even. "They're still asleep right now, actually, so I'm trying to keep the noise down. They were up late watching movies."

"I see," Jocelyn said. "You didn't stop by to tell me how things were with the house, so I wanted to find out how that had gone."

Ella felt instantly remorseful at her irritation. Of course Jocelyn would be interested in news about Neil's house. She'd completely for-gotten to give her an update yesterday. "It's in bad shape," she said. "The tenants have gone, but they left a huge mess behind them. It's going to be expensive to fix it all up again."

Jocelyn's hands flew up. "Oh, that's awful!" she said. "And they just ran off and left it like that? Can you sue them? Make them pay for the damage? Oh, that beautiful house!"

"I'll talk to the estate agent on Monday and he'll walk me through what options I have," Ella said. "To be honest, I wonder whether I shouldn't just sell it. I don't think I'm cut out to be a landlord."

"Sell Neil's house?" Jocelyn screeched. "It was his pride and joy! I'm sure he would have wanted you to keep it to pass on to Tiffany."

Ella clamped her mouth shut. Of course, Jocelyn would be fixated on Neil's imaginary legacy, propping up her idol no matter what it cost, or what the practicalities of the situation demanded. "We'll see," Ella said through gritted teeth.

"Oh, you poor thing!" Jocelyn leaned forward and hugged Ella's stiff body. "Well, let me know what happens. See you soon."

Jocelyn headed toward her house, and Ella closed the door behind her. She'd woken up feeling rested and happy. She refused to let Jocelyn's words wreck that.

She finished tidying up the living room and had mixed up a batch of pancake batter when the bedroom door opened and Tiffany came out, rubbing her eyes. "Morning, Mum. I thought I smelled pancakes."

Ella laughed. "I've barely started making them! Did you have a good sleep?"

Sophie appeared in the doorway and stood next to Tiffany. Ella looked from one sleepy face to the other. They could almost be sisters with their tawny skin and dark brown curls.

Ella turned to the cooker, where she had four frying pans on the go, each with one pancake. She turned them over one by one, revealing the golden-brown side.

"I love pancakes!" Sophie said. The girls came up to the counter and climbed onto the bar stools.

"Good, because I'm making plenty," Ella said. She put the pancakes onto a plate and poured more batter into the pans. "Wash up and grab yourselves some plates."

The girls wasted no time washing their hands and getting back into their seats. Ella gave each one a pancake. Tiffany had hers with chocolate spread while Sophie wanted honey. Ella had just finished stacking the third batch of four onto a plate when they heard a knock on the door.

She turned off the gas burners and pulled open the front door. Ragnar stood there freshly shaven, hair slightly damp. She caught a hint of his aftershave and was thrown for a moment. Ambergris and patchouli... It smelled exactly like the cologne she used to buy for Neil. The one he used to wear in the early days of their marriage. Something must have registered in her face, because Ragnar's smile flickered.

She shook herself mentally and said, "Hi, Ragnar! Come in. The girls just got up. They're having breakfast."

"Smells good," he said, following her into the house.

"Hi, Dad!" Sophie called out.

"You're welcome to join in," Ella said. "But better hurry because I can't promise there'll be any left if you hang about too long."

"Thank you!" he said.

She got a side plate and some cutlery and put them on the counter. The girls cleared away and went off to Tiffany's room.

"What do you like on your pancakes?" Ella asked. "We've got chocolate spread, honey, jam, and lemon juice."

"Lemon and sugar," he said. "Anything else is sacrilege."

Ella laughed. "There you go."

As he sprinkled caster sugar on a warm pancake she said, "Sorry I zonked out last night. That's not how I normally entertain my guests."

"I accept your apology," he said, his face solemn. "I've never been so insulted in my life. I know I don't possess the most sparkling wit, but I never thought I'd bore a person to sleep."

Embarrassed, she opened her mouth to reply and noticed that the corners of his mouth were turned up, and his eyes twinkled. She smiled, and he grinned back.

"Seriously, it's fine," he went on. "You clearly needed the rest and I'm glad you got it. I really enjoyed the movies and popcorn."

"Thanks. Me too. Thankfully, I don't need to make a decision about that whole wretched business until next week."

"How bad was it?" he asked, then added quickly, "If you don't mind telling me. It's fine if you don't want to talk about it."

"No, I don't mind," she said. "It's really filthy. Some of the light fixtures were torn out. I didn't check whether the appliances still worked. There were holes in the walls as well."

"Does your agent think it's mostly malicious damage as opposed to wear and tear?" he asked.

"What's the difference?"

"A long time ago, I used to manage property," he said. "You'd have to be able to distinguish between what damage was caused by deliberate action and what came about due to normal wear and tear."

"My agent said he would walk me through my options on Monday," Ella said. "I had insurance and I'm hoping that the tenants' deposit will cover some of the repairs, but we still don't know what the full price tag for it all will be."

"It really stinks," Ragnar said. "Even if you did have landlord's insurance, sometimes there can be a whole song and dance about whether certain things constitute separate claims and are subject to a separate excess fee." He winced and added, "Even with all that, you may still end up out of pocket. I don't want to be pessimistic, and we will pray for the best outcome, of course, but it's good to be prepared."

Ella sighed. "Not what I wanted to hear, but I appreciate your honesty."

"There's a lot of risk involved in being a landlord," he said. "Basically because people can be idiots."

Ella laughed. "Idiots cause most of the world's problems. And, sadly, they don't all come wearing a sign."

His face was serious again. "I'd like to help, if there's anything I can do. I know a really great contractor who's worked for me in the past."

Warmth spread inside her chest. "I really appreciate that. I'll hear what the estate agent says on Monday, then let you know."
After breakfast, Ragnar and Sophie headed back home. Ella stood at the door and waved at them while they crossed the road, Sophie skipping ahead, still in her pajamas. Ella's

smile lingered for a while. The day felt a lot brighter.

Chapter Thirteen

RAGNAR WHISTLED AS he ran a duster over his bookshelves.

Sophie, standing with an armful of toys on her way to the toy box, looked at him, her head slightly tilted. "Are you happy Dad?"

"Hmm? What?"

"You only whistle like that when you're happy," she said. "Are you happy?"

Ragnar smiled. "I suppose I am."

"Me too," Sophie said. "I'm happy because I have a best friend. But I can't whistle."

"I'll have to teach you how. It's the perfect thing for happy people to do," he said.

"I really love Tiffany. And I really love Ella. I love having neighbors."

"Yes, they are great, aren't they?" Ragnar said, working the duster into a corner of the windowsill. "We need to hurry up. We want to get this place tidy before your uncle Magnus and Aunt Nia get here."

"Yeah," Sophie said, and dumped her toys into a box in the corner of the room. "Are they coming soon?"

"Any minute," Ragnar answered. He looked around the room. He had a cleaner who came in once a week to handle the most significant jobs in the house, but it never ceased to amaze him how much easier it was to make a mess than to clean it up. Especially after Sophie and Tiffany had spent the day here yesterday making forts with all the soft furnishing and playing with all of

Sophie's favorite toys. It had been wonderful to see how much fun they had together. The whole day had been great. The afternoon with the girls, then the evening watching movies with them and Ella.

Then this morning at breakfast... He silently echoed Sophie's thankfulness about their new neighbors. What an incredible blessing it was.

He saw Magnus's dark blue SUV pull up, but before he could say anything, Sophie yelled, "Here they are!"

She ran to the front door and pulled it open, hopping from foot to foot. Ragnar walked up behind her and watched as his brother and sister-in-law got out of their car.

Magnus Klassen laughed and scooped up his niece. "Hello, little munchkin." He glanced at Ragnar. "Hey, big munchkin."

"Hello yourself," Ragnar said. "Out of the way while I talk to civilized people." He hugged Magnus's wife Nia, once again struck by her effortless beauty. She had always been a striking woman, but she looked especially radiant today in a peacock blue kaftan that set off the coppery undertones of her terracotta-colored skin.

"Come on in," he said, moving aside so Sophie could get a cuddle from her aunt.

"You look like a princess, Auntie Nia," Sophie said.

Nia laughed. "Thank you! You're looking adorable yourself. I love your hair."

Sophie put her hand up to her curls, which were plaited in neat cornrows. "Ella did it. She's really good with hair. She's my childminder and Tiffany is my best friend."

"Oh, this is your neighbor," Nia said, glancing at Ragnar. "How's all that going?"

"Really well," Ragnar said. "She's been a godsend."

Sophie was eager to chat with her aunt and uncle, so Ragnar busied himself getting lunch set up on the dining table. The quiche was store-bought but good, and he could make a decent salad. Marriage clearly suited his younger brother, Ragnar thought. Magnus looked relaxed and happy, his eyes never straying far from his wife's face.

After dessert, Sophie took Nia upstairs to inspect her new dollhouse while Magnus helped Ragnar ferry the dishes into the kitchen. "How's Theta Software?" Magnus asked. "Handover going okay?"

"Yes, everyone's being extremely cooperative and efficient."

"Any thoughts about what you'll do when you've handed over the reins?" Magnus kept his tone light and his eyes averted.

Ragnar laughed. "Don't worry. I'm not going to fly halfway around the world again or do anything crazy." He knew how worried his family had been last year when, soon after his brother's wedding, he'd made a spur-of-the-moment decision to leave his business in the hands of his partners and take off on an indefinite leave of absence. Magnus had asked whether he was having some kind of a breakdown and, in hindsight, Ragnar supposed he had been.

But it was over now, and he was feeling better than he'd been for a long time. He felt like the pieces of his life were coming back together. For the first time since Zuri had gone, he was spending more time looking forward with hope instead of backward with regret. Sophie was thriving and settled, thrilled to have made a good friend. It all had to do with his new neighbors across the road.

Magnus watched him closely. "You would tell me if anything was up, right?"

"Of course. I'm fine. Really. In answer to your previous question, I'm not entirely sure what I'll do. It won't be the same line of business because I agreed to a non-compete clause. Maybe I'll come asking you for a job. Isn't business booming?"

Magnus laughed. "Yes, we're doing great. And that may not be such a bad idea. The topic of biologics discovery is coming up a lot lately as we think about our next steps, and we might want to go in that direction. I wouldn't mind picking your brain a bit."

Ragnar raised his eyebrows. "That does sound interesting. It's using software engineering to develop new drugs, right?"

"Shop talk?" Nia said, stepping into the kitchen. "I leave you alone for five minutes and you just can't help yourselves."

She walked up to Magnus's side and he wrapped his arm around her shoulders. "Seriously, though, I don't want to interrupt," she said.

Magnus said, "No, it's fine. Actually, now that you're here, do you think it's a good time to tell Ragnar our news?"

Magnus and Nia exchanged a look and Ragnar knew in an instant what the news was, even before Nia nodded her head and Magnus said, "You're going to be an uncle."

A flood of emotions crashed over Ragnar in distinct waves. Delight for his brother. Surprise. And pain. A gnawing ache welling up inside because this was yet another experience Zuri was missing. She would have been thrilled for Magnus.

"Wow! That's wonderful," he managed to say, pulling them both into a hug. He stepped back, swiping at the moisture in his eyes. "That quiche had too many onions." Magnus and Nia laughed.

"Seriously, mate, that's awesome," Ragnar said. "When?"

"September or October," Magnus said.

"We'd have told you earlier, but you were still abroad, and we really wanted to let you know face to face," Nia added.

"Can I tell Sophie? Do you know what you're having?" Ragnar asked.

"Not yet," Magnus said. "Nia wants to find out, but I want the surprise. We've got an ultrasound coming up next week and they should be able to tell, if the little fellow cooperates. You can tell Sophie after that."

Ragnar kept a smile on his face even as a spasm of pain squeezed his chest. "We" have an ultrasound. He'd not gone for Sophie's ultrasound. He'd been tied up in a business meeting. He couldn't even remember what the meeting had been about, but he had thought it important enough not to attend the scan with Zuri. One of the many things that had seemed so urgent back then and which he'd given a higher priority than what he should have known was his real treasure. What a blind fool he'd been.

"Okay. Great!" he forced out. "I really am happy for you guys. Hang on." He reached up to a high shelf and pulled down three Royal Scot Crystal glasses. "This definitely calls for a toast." He filled them with apple juice and passed one each to Magnus and Nia.

Holding up his own, he said, "To Magnus, Nia, and the little fellow. Blessings, joy, and long life." They clinked glasses. He didn't try to hide the moisture in his eyes.

Ragnar put his glass down and hugged his brother, slapping his back. "Congratulations. Enjoy the moment. You never know how long you've got."

Chapter Fourteen

CROSS THE ROAD at Jocelyn's house, Ella passed the Yorkshire puddings to Jarvis, not managing to get her hand away before he caressed her fingers. She resisted the urge to impale his hand with her fork. He smirked at her and helped himself to two puddings, then covered them with a generous helping of gravy.

Jocelyn revisited the topic she hadn't been able to stray far from all afternoon. "I still can't believe those awful tenants of yours. How could they do that?"

"Utterly shameful," Jarvis put in. "This estate agent of yours sounds a bit useless. Hasn't he been carrying out inspections? Bad enough to have been hoodwinked into leasing the house, but he should have been able to spot this sort of nonsense months ago."

Ella didn't say anything. She hated talking about her business in front of that man.

Jocelyn said, "Not to mention the rent arrears. This isn't the first time they've done this."

"You're joking." Jarvis listened with relish as Jocelyn dived into an account of the first time Ella's tenants had been late with their rent. When Jocelyn finished recounting the tale, Jarvis shook his head. "That agent of yours is having a laugh, Ella. Are you sure you can trust him to handle the rest of this business? You've got a four-bed house next to Priory Park in Reigate. You should be raking in the cash, not being fleeced like this. What's your agent's name?"

"I'm perfectly happy with my agent," Ella said, remembering how gentle and kind Charles had been, despite his stiff formality. "I'm confident that he knows what he's doing."

Jarvis scoffed and Jocelyn said, "Sweetheart, I think Jarvis has a point. This agent hasn't exactly done a good job so far. And that house is your only asset. It's poor Neil's legacy to his daughter. When I think of how hard he worked, how proud he was when you moved in there, it just breaks my heart." Her eyes filled with tears, and Jarvis circled his arm around her shoulders.

Ella poked at her food, glad that Tiffany had been excused from the table and was in the other room. It might be unreasonable, she thought, but she didn't like her daughter seeing Jocelyn crying. Still, the woman had a right to grieve her son.

"I know, Jocelyn. I'll hear what the agent has to tell me on Monday." She stood up and began to collect the dinner plates.

"You poor dear. And then you're doing all this on your own as well. People just see a young woman like you and think they can take advantage. It can be hard taking care of all this without a man around," Jocelyn said. She suddenly sat up straight. "You know what? Jarvis has connections. Maybe he knows somebody who could advise you."

"I'd be happy to help," Jarvis said, baring his teeth.

Ella picked up a stack of plates and walked toward the kitchen. "Thanks for the offer, but I'm okay. Charles is on top of it." She set the plates down at the sink and went back to the table to get some more. Jocelyn thanked her for her help and headed off to the living room to find out what Tiffany was doing.

Ella placed some more dishes onto the counter. She felt a presence looming up behind her and whirled around to see Jarvis standing close by, his eyes fixed on her. He stepped closer, into her personal space. She tried to move backward but felt the counter digging into her back. Jarvis leered. "Jocelyn is right, you know. It's such a shame that you're all alone, handling all these problems on your own. You need a man."

His eyes devoured her, and he moved even closer, so close that she could feel his hot moist breath on her cheek as he murmured. "Yes, Ella. You need a man."

"Excuse me, Jarvis. I need to get past," she said.

He didn't budge. "I'm happy to help."

"I said no, thanks." She held up her hands and pushed past him into the dining room. She could hear him chuckling.

"Tiffany, sweetheart, it's time to go home," she called out. Should she tell Jocelyn about Jarvis? But what would she say? He would insist that all he had said was he wanted to help her. He was repeating Jocelyn's own words about her needing a man to help her. She knew that he'd taken those words and twisted them to fit his own intentions, but how could she explain that to Jocelyn? Her mother-in-law's blind spots were man-sized, especially when that man happened to be one close to her.

As Jocelyn came back into the dining room with Tiffany, Jarvis said, "Remember, the offer stands."

Jocelyn said, "Are you going already, sweetheart? I thought you'd stay a bit longer. And you really should consider taking Jarvis up on his offer. He really wants to help, and I'm sure he'd soon set things to rights."

Ella didn't turn to look at the smirk she knew would be on Jarvis's face. "I'll see you soon, Jocelyn."

"Let me know how it goes on Monday," she said.

Ella thanked her and ignored Jarvis's farewell as she hustled Tiffany out of the house.

Her skin crawled at the memory of Jarvis so close to her, breathing on her cheek. She wanted to take a shower and wash him off. Even if she was able to tell Jocelyn her suspicions, her mother-in-law would never believe her, besotted as she was with Jarvis. In Jocelyn's eyes, the sun rose and set on Jarvis, and he could do no wrong.

She had been the same with Neil. He was her golden boy. Ella remembered how endlessly Jocelyn would gush about Neil. That's what made it so hard to tell her that the boy she idolized was far from perfect. Very far. Ella had thought that the kindest thing to do was let Jocelyn keep her precious memories of her son and not burden her with the truth about his many failings.

She let herself and Tiffany into their apartment and looked around the small entryway and through to the living room. Their home. Thanks to Jocelyn, she had a place to live. She didn't pay rent, but living here had its price. Jocelyn was well-meaning but meddlesome, and with her came Jarvis.

Ella pictured the months and years ahead, living under Jocelyn's nose, Jarvis hovering in the background, trying his luck whenever he got the chance. She shuddered. There had to be a way out of this.

Chapter Fifteen

MONDAY AFTERNOON WAS one of those perfect sun-drenched spring days when the greenery was still bright and fresh and the flowers of the season were in full bloom. Ella grinned as Tiffany and Sophie skipped ahead through the entry gates to Leeds Castle. She wanted to skip right along with them. It felt like stepping into a fairytale, a place where knights in shining armor still rode off on brave quests, a world away from the reality of shady tenants and trashed houses.

She looked up and saw Ragnar was smiling as well as he walked beside her. "Amazing, isn't it? Like another world."

"That's exactly what I was thinking," she said. Coming here had been Ragnar's idea. He'd volunteered to take a day off and watch Tiffany while she met with her estate agent in the morning. Since the weather forecast was promising, he suggested that they drive over to Kent and visit what was marketed as "the loveliest castle in the world." Ella agreed eagerly; she had wanted to come here for years.

They hadn't reached the castle itself but were matching the girls' pace as the children dawdled and frolicked around the extensive grounds.

Ragnar studied the illustrated map they picked up at the ticket office. "We want to tour the castle proper, of course," he said.

"They've also got a maze with a grotto underneath and a playground. There's a falconry demonstration and a miniature railroad, and we could go punting on the river."

"I want to do all of it," Ella said, "but I don't think we'll manage it in a couple of hours."

"The tickets are valid for a year, so we could always come back any time over the next twelve months."

Ella's heart rate quickened at the thought of visiting this place again with Ragnar. "Really? Um, okay." She looked at the girls, who had taken another detour off the path to check out a patch of daffodils. "At the pace they're going, exploring inch by inch, we'll need about that long to see all of it." She looked around and took a deep breath. "But you can't rush a place like this. It's nice to just soak it all in."

They paused, waiting for the girls. "So, you've never been here before?" Ella asked.

"No. My wife talked about coming, but the timing was never right. Crazy, since we're not that far away."

Ella liked the thought that they were sharing an experience that was the first for them both. The girls darted back onto the path and ran on ahead.

Ragnar said, "Now that they're out of earshot, give me the full story. What did your estate agent have to say?"

Ella smiled. "You were right about pretty much every point. He'll claim their deposit for all the malicious damage. And it turns out the insurance cover pays for everything. I have fittings and fixtures insurance, tenant default insurance, and I've also got legal protection if I decide to go after them for the rent arrears."

"That's wonderful!" Ragnar said. "Sounds like you got yourself an incredible agent."

"I know!" Ella said. "He's really formal, almost pedantic, and I thought it was overkill getting all of that cover at the time. But he really knows what he's doing. I'm so grateful to God that it all seems to be working out."

"I've been praying that it would," Ragnar said. "Having any property trashed is awful enough, but it must have been even more devastating since it was the home where you and your husband lived."

He paused for a moment then asked, "Was it hard to move away from there after losing him?"

Ella's mouth twisted in a wry smile. "Everything was hard. Moving was hard. Staying would have been just as hard. But it wasn't an option."

"One thing that surprised me was how busy death is," Ragnar said. "You've got so much to sort through, so many people to tell, official agencies to inform, things to organize."

"I was actually glad I had so much to do," Ella said. "It meant that I didn't have to stop and think. It got hardest for me when everything was done, and everyone had gone back to their regular lives—"

"And you're left with this big empty gap," Ragnar concluded. "And people don't know what to say to you."

"I know!" Ella said. "And they tell you things like, 'Just let me know if there's anything I can do for you.' I get it, I know they mean well, but I was so numb and overwhelmed that I couldn't even think of what kind of help to ask for."

"That's exactly how I felt," Ragnar said. "I think what blessed me most was when my brother would just come and do things without asking. He'd take Sophie off to the playground so I could have some time to switch off. Or he'd come over with a big bag of groceries. Fill up the freezer with frozen ready meals. I don't know whether he ever realized how much that helped me. And I shouldn't forget my little sister Vanya. She would just come over and hang out and not try to get me do anything."

"That is really sweet," Ella said. "People generally do try their best." She thought of Jocelyn in the immediate aftermath of Neil's death. Her mother-in-law had collapsed under the shock of losing her only child, and Ella had found herself taking on the burden of managing Jocelyn's grief as well as her own.

In many ways, she still was, she thought.

"I don't know what I'd have done without my family," Ragnar said.

"Sounds like you're really close."

He smiled. "We are. It's made all the difference for Sophie and me. Did you have family to help you after Neil died?"

Ella shook her head. "My mother passed away years ago when I was just out of my teens. And my father was never in my life. He…" she hesitated for a moment. "He was married to someone else when he was involved with my mum. And when she turned up pregnant, her family wanted nothing to do with her. So, it was pretty much just us."

"I'm sorry," he said. The sympathy in his eyes wrenched at her heart. "You've lost so much."

She managed a smile. "It sounds pathetic when I say it, but, honestly, I've got a lot to be thankful for.

Mum was amazing and I only have good memories from my childhood. She moved to a different part of the country and found a great church community who became her new support network."

He was about to speak when the girls came running back. "We're hungry," Tiffany said. "Are we going to have our lunch now?"

Ragnar looked at Ella. "I guess we could. Shall we look for some picnic tables or just find a spot on the grass?"

"That looks nice," Ella said, pointing at an expanse of green lawn on a gently rising hill. "We could put our blankets down there."

The girls ran off in the direction she was pointing.

An elderly couple walking toward them smiled at the girls. The lady looked at Ella and laughed. "I wish I had their energy!"

"I'd be fine with even half of it!" Ella said.

She and Ragnar followed the girls onto the lawn and spread out their picnic blankets.

Ragnar took a long deep breath and drank in the breathtaking view of the castle as it rose from the moat. Why had it taken him so many years to come see it when it was less than an hour from his home? Better late than never, though. And being here today, right now, felt like the perfect moment to share with Sophie. His gaze strayed to Ella, who was making a daisy chain for his daughter. She was part of what was making this moment perfect. This amazing woman whose nurturing gentleness was bringing so much joy and healing to his daughter.

Ella placed the chain over Sophie's head, and Sophie flung her arms around Ella's neck. Ella smiled and hugged the child back. Ragnar's heart swelled with thankfulness that she was in his and Sophie's life right now. Thankfulness and something more. Something deeper. An aching longing so powerful and sudden that it caught him by surprise. "Ella."

He hadn't realized that he had spoken her name out loud until she looked at him expectantly.

He blinked and stammered, scrambling for something to say. "Um, uh... What shall we see next?"

Ella picked up the map and traced a line with her finger. "If we follow this path, we'll get to the castle first. Then we can go on to the Culpeper Gardens and get to the maze and finally the playground."

"With all the various distractions along the way," Ragnar said. "Let's get on, then."

They packed up the picnic things and meandered along the path. They took a tour of the castle, once an ancient Norman stronghold which Henry VIII had had renovated for his first wife, Catherine of Aragon. Sophie and Tiffany hurried them through, more interested in getting back outside than lingering in the state rooms and soaking in the castle's nine-hundred-year history.

The girls were delighted with the maze and the deliciously creepy grotto underneath. By the time they got to the Knight's Stronghold Playground, designed to look like a castle, it was late afternoon.

"There's so much we haven't managed to see," Ella said. "We'll just have to come back another day."

The girls were reluctant to leave, but the promise of a future visit made it easier to bear. The miniature train had taken its last trip of the day, so they had to make the long way back to the exit on foot.

"I'm so tired," Tiffany grumbled.

"Me too," Sophie echoed.

The girls took turns riding piggyback on Ragnar. The gates were closed for the day, and they had to go through the gift shop to get to the parking lot. Tiffany and Sophie forgot their exhaustion as they browsed through the shop's large selection of toys, costumes, and souvenirs. Ella leafed through the glossy pages of a coffee table book while Ragnar inspected the build-your-own-castle toy models. An elderly lady bumped into Ragnar, then apologized.

"No, no problem at all," Ragnar said. It was the same lady they had passed earlier on the path.

The woman gestured at the girls. "You've got such beautiful daughters. Are they twins?"

Taken aback, Ragnar stammered, "Um, no. No, they're not."

"Well, they're lovely and they get along so well and play so nicely together," the lady went on. "I've been seeing you about all this afternoon, and those girls are a real credit to you and your wife."

Ella had looked up, and Ragnar saw her freeze.

The lady patted Ella's arm and nodded at Ragnar. "These are really precious years. Enjoy them. Make the most of them."

"Thanks!" Ragnar said, not wanting to embarrass the woman by explaining her mistake. The lady smiled and headed out of the shop.

Ella was suddenly absorbed in listening to Tiffany's chatter about a small souvenir she wanted. Ella agreed to buy a small teddy bear wearing a T-shirt with the castle crest while Ragnar bought a matching one for Sophie.

Ella stowed the picnic blankets in the trunk of the car while Ragnar helped the girls get strapped in. Both looked tired but happy, their cheeks flushed with exercise and sunshine. He could see why the woman had thought the children were sisters with their parents on a family outing. With their hair plaited in the same cornrowed style and their similar coloring, it was an easy assumption to make.

And, like everything else on this perfect day, it all seemed to fit, as though a blurry picture he'd been squinting at had suddenly clicked into focus.

Chapter Sixteen

RAGNAR BREATHED A prayer of thanks that the glorious weather had continued through the week and into the bank holiday weekend. He had invited Magnus, Nia, and his sister Vanya to a barbecue in his back yard. Ella and Tiffany would be coming, too. Since the day out at Leeds Castle, a new hope and a new prayer had begun to grow in his heart. It was a secret too deep and delicate to whisper to anyone else but his God. But he had caught a glimpse of it that sunny afternoon, like a snatch of the tail end of a beautiful dream he wanted to grasp and cling onto before it vanished.

Having Ella and Tiffany meet his family wasn't exactly a test, but he sensed that it would tell him more about whether he had grounds for hope, or whether it was all just an ephemeral dream.

He hadn't mentioned to his family who else was invited, and although he had told Ella he was having people over, he had not told her exactly which people. He wondered now whether that had been a mistake. But it was too late to backtrack. It was done, and all he could do was pray that God would excuse his blunders.

Magnus, Nia and Vanya arrived mid-morning, and Vanya and Sophie were now playing Jenga with a set of super-sized wooden blocks on the freshly mowed lawn. Ragnar tinkered with the grill, checking the temperature and the progress of the meat and vegetables under the hood.

Nia came outside from the kitchen, holding a bowl of potato salad. She set it down next to the other dishes. "I'm going to put my feet up now," she declared, heading over next to the table where Magnus was lining up drinks and glasses.

Ragnar said, "Yes, please do take a load off. We've got everything well in hand." He looked at her more closely. "Are you feeling okay?" Magnus had told him that Nia was struggling with morning sickness, and he wondered whether the strong smells of barbecuing food bothered her.

"I'm fine. Just sleepy!" she said. "I could easily doze off right here. Where are the rest of your guests? I don't want them to catch me snoring."

"They should be here any minute," Ragnar said, just as the doorbell chimed. "Perfect timing."

His heart thudded heavily as he went back into the house and through to the front door. Ella smiled up at him from his front doorstep, looking stunning in a pale blue sun dress that draped her body in modest and yet beautifully feminine lines. She held up a dish. "I brought a raspberry tart."

"Thanks," he said, taking the pie. "You look delicious. No, it! I mean it does." His face felt hot as he pointed. "The tart looks delicious. Come in! Hi, Tiffany."

He let them walk past him and said, "Go straight into the back yard." He was right behind them as Tiffany ran out toward Sophie and Ella stepped onto the deck. Magnus straightened up and Nia's eyes widened as she swung her feet off the deck chair.

"Ella, this is my brother Magnus, my sister-in-law Nia, and my sister Vanya. Guys, this is Ella from across the road."

Ella froze for a heartbeat. Nia rushed forward, arms extended. "So, you're the one Sophie won't stop talking about. It's lovely to meet you!" She pulled Ella into a hug.

Magnus held out his hand. "Hi! Did you make that tart my brother's trying to palm off as his?"

"I did," Ella said, her cheeks dimpling in a smile. "It's nice to meet you. And I understand congratulations are in order. Ragnar told me you're getting a new arrival this autumn."

Nia smiled. "Thank you! I can't tell you what we're having because somebody is determined to keep the surprise." She jerked her thumb toward Magnus. "So I'm keeping all the non-neutral baby gear hidden away."

"I don't want to ruin the suspense," Magnus said. He asked Ella, "Did you find out ahead of time with your daughter?"

"Of course I did," Ella said. "But then I'm the kind who always flips to the back of a book to check the ending. I like my surprises early."

Vanya came over from the Jenga game and said hi, then steered Ella over to a seat under the large umbrella.

Ragnar hung back while his sister settled Ella and offered her a cold drink. It seemed to be going okay. Maybe his little experiment bringing Ella together with his family wouldn't backfire after all.

Ella sat between Nia and Vanya, half her brain making polite chit-chat while the other half tried to wrap itself around the shock of who Ragnar's guests were. What did he mean by springing them on her? Or her on them? Maybe she shouldn't read anything into it. He, she and the girls had fallen into the habit of spending a lot of time together, so it seemed natural that he'd ask her and Tiffany over. It just happened to coincide with a barbecue when his family was visiting. It was nothing.

She wondered what sort of impression she was making. Did they like her? Did she look okay? She was only wearing an old sun dress she'd picked up on sale from the supermarket last summer. Vanya's makeup and clothes were immaculate, and Nia's outfit must have cost a fortune.

She relaxed a bit more as they talked. It was always easy to chat about babies, and Nia was eager to pick her brain about the pros and cons of natural childbirth versus epidurals and other medication. Vanya was a lot quieter, but she seemed friendly and interested.

Then she caught Ragnar watching her. When she snagged his eyes the first time, he looked away quickly, but the second time it happened, he smiled at her, and warmth spread throughout her body. From then on, she had a growing awareness of his gaze on her.

Her mind continued to revolve. This lunch, with his family and the way he was looking at her... the contours of the puzzle pieces sharpened and started to fit into place. Her stomach churned and she wondered whether she'd be able to eat anything, although the food smelled amazing. Her mouth felt dry, but she didn't trust herself to pick up her glass of juice without knocking it over.

"I think you'd better check those steaks," Magnus said to his brother. Ella glanced up just as Ragnar turned his eyes away from her, his face turning brick red.

"Oh! Right." He slid a batch of well-done steaks onto a serving platter while Magnus made a joke about not planning on eating burnt offerings.

She excused herself and went to the bathroom, leaning against the door while she pressed her hands against her hot cheeks.

Friendship with Ragnar was comfortable, like a well-used warm blanket. But beyond friendship was an area of her heart that she had closed and sealed off two years ago. At least she thought she had sealed it off. The last time she'd let someone in there, he had broken her, smashed her into such tiny bits that she wasn't sure if she could ever be whole again.

Was this friendship turning into something else? Did she want it to? She knew how easy it would be to let her heart and her imagination run wild, to give in to the deep undercurrents she had read in his eyes as he looked at her, and which she knew could all-too-easily find their match in her own heart. She'd let herself be swept away once before.

She went to the sink and washed her hands, aware that the minutes were passing and she should go back out before it began to look strange. A verse from the Song of Solomon sprang into her mind. *"I charge you, O daughters of Jerusalem, do not stir up nor awaken love until it pleases."* Love awakened at the wrong time and with the wrong man only brought heartache. She didn't even want to think about going down that road until she'd had a lot more time to calm herself, to think, and pray.

Ella was the first to leave that evening, taking a reluctant but exhausted Tiffany back across the road to their home.

When they left, Nia volunteered to read a bedtime story for Sophie, and the two went upstairs to choose a book. While Vanya was busy in the kitchen, Ragnar and his brother tidied up the back yard.

Magnus cleared his throat as he folded up the large garden umbrella. "So, um, are you and Ella seeing a lot of each other?"

Ragnar shot him a look. Magnus had not wasted any time. "She's taking care of my daughter. So, yes, I see her quite often."

"Not everyone invites their child-minder to hang out, though," Magnus pointed out.

"Fair enough. Okay, she's more than a child-minder. I'd consider her a friend. I'm getting to know her a bit, and so far, I like what I'm seeing."

Magnus said slowly, "The last time you met an attractive single woman who you considered a friend, I found myself getting measured for a best man's suit."

Ragnar felt his face reddening.

Magnus said, "For what it's worth, I like her. She seems sweet. And it's clear Sophie adores her as well. I'm not getting any sort of predatory or opportunistic vibe from her, if that's what you're worried about."

Ragnar's head jerked up. "Opportunistic? What are you talking about?"

"I mean you're quite a catch," Magnus said. Ragnar scoffed, but

Magnus went on. "I'm serious. Anyone who throws your name into a search engine doesn't have to go past the first page of results to find out that you've made a killing in your business. And there's that Klassen name. It attracts a certain kind of woman like bees to honey."

"That sounds like something Father would say," Ragnar said.

Magnus winced. Being compared to Karl Klassen was not a compliment. "Ouch. I don't normally agree with Father, but even a stopped clock is correct twice a day. Anyway, I'm not seeing that sort of thing with Ella. Nia's much better than I am at reading people, but I think Ella's a good person to have in your life right now. At the very least, she's good for your daughter. Anything beyond that, well, I can't say I'm an expert at this. I was definitely punching above my weight when I got Nia."

Ragnar laughed. "True. I have no idea what she sees in you." He pulled the waterproof cover over the barbecue. "But thanks. I appreciate your thoughts. And to be honest, that's why I wanted you to meet her. I feel like I can't think straight. I just feel so... empty. Like a huge part of me was ripped away. I won't lie: I'm very attracted to Ella. She's beautiful in so many ways, and I'm not just talking about the outside. But I don't want to just grab onto the next likely-looking warm body and try to use her to plug up a void. I've had chances to do that, and I've been tempted to. Not with Ella, but while I was traveling. But I know the mess that would cause, how much harm comes when we step outside the boundaries God has set. But I haven't said anything to her about how I feel, and I don't want to run ahead of myself. For all I know, she may not even see me that way at all. I want to be sure that a future with her is what's best for all of us. I want to know whether it's in God's plan for us."

Magnus was silent for a moment as he secured the umbrella. He looked up at Ragnar. "I don't have any answers for you. But I'll pray. We'll pray, if you're okay with me telling Nia."

"Thanks," Ragnar said. He hadn't intended being so frank with his brother. But he was glad he had.

Chapter Seventeen

ELLA SANK INTO her sofa after she said good night to Tiffany. With her daughter asleep, she was free to surrender her mind to the storm of thoughts that had been raging in her head all afternoon and evening.

She'd measured the situation from every angle she could think of, and her conclusion was the same every time: Ragnar was interested in her. Until today, all the time they'd spent together—and that had been a lot—had been about the girls. But having her meet his family felt like he was intentionally stepping things up. Wasn't that supposed to be one of the telltale signs that a man was getting serious about a relationship?

She stopped shying away from the thought and allowed her mind to go there. What would it be like to have Ragnar in her life? In one sense he was already in her life. He'd become a constant presence over the past months. She took care of his daughter all through the week, and they always had a chat when he came across the road to get Sophie.

As the weather warmed up, they often went on outings with the girls, exploring the countryside and historical buildings. They went to the same small church every Sunday. But what would it be like if they were a real family? Tiffany would love having a sister, and Ragnar was a far better dad than Neil had ever been.

And herself? Could she imagine having a husband again? Her mouth felt dry and her heart hammered faster as she tried the thought on for size. Her friendship with Ragnar had grown naturally, like a slow and gradual sunrise. It hadn't been like the whirlwind of her first months with Neil, when he'd pursued her with a single-minded and over-whelming intensity that turned her world upside down. Spinning around in Neil's orbit had exhilarated her but left her off-balance. And everything had revolved around Neil, such was the force of his powerful gravitational pull.

As for physical attraction, there was no question that Ragnar was good-looking. She'd seen that immediately. But Neil had been even more handsome, and that had counted for nothing in the end. By the time of his accident, she'd barely even registered the charms that had once been so captivating.

She had gotten things so badly wrong with Neil that she no longer trusted her radar, couldn't trust in her ability to detect a good man, to separate the gold from the dross. What if she were focusing on the wrong things again? What if there were big red flags that she was missing? With hindsight, she could now see the danger signals that had been right in her face about Neil. But when you were in the middle of being swept off your feet by a hurricane, the last thing you wanted to do is sit down and analyze it.

She was done with being swept off her feet, thank you very much. She wanted to stay firmly on the ground. And now, she had far more important things to worry about than her own heart. Ella's eyes strayed to the doorway of her daughter's room. If she chose to let the wrong man into her life again, Tiffany could be hurt. She had once gambled her heart away and lost; she was not going to take any chances with her child's welfare.

Ella closed her eyes and prayed. *Lord, I don't know what's going on with Ragnar. I don't even know whether I'm being presumptuous. This might all just be nothing, and maybe my imagination is running away with me and he's just being a friendly neighbor. I like him. Fine, I admit it: I like him a lot. Help me to discern what is true and to know how to relate to him. I don't trust my own ability to see clearly because I got it so badly wrong before. Give me enough light for the next step, and please help me not to blunder again.*

As she continued to pray, she felt her tension ease and her troubled heart quiet down into serenity.

Chapter Eighteen

A COUPLE OF weeks later, after dropping Tiffany off at her Sunday School room, Ella headed to the adults' class. She was looking forward to today's lesson. They were going through the book of James. Her friend Macey Travis was loitering with intent outside the door.

Macey gave her a quick hug. "Do you have a moment?"

"Right now?" Ella asked. "Won't we be late? The class is about to start."

"I know," Macey said. "But this is important."

"All right," Ella said. She scanned Macey's face, but she couldn't read her expression. Macey linked arms with her and they walked down the corridor and turned in to the cafeteria.

The room was empty apart from a couple of volunteers who were setting things up for the coffee and snacks that would be served after the Sunday school classes were over. Macey steered Ella over to a table in the farthest corner of the room, where they sat down.

Macey cleared her throat. "So, um, how are things going with the house?"

Ella gave her friend a double-take. "The house? The repairs are pretty much done. My estate agent says he'll soon be able to list it again, once I sign off on everything."

"Great! Good to hear it."

Ella stared at Macey. "You pulled me away from Sunday School to talk about my house repairs?"

Macey met her eyes. "No. You know me, Ella. I always call a spade a spade, but I've been struggling to work up the courage to ask. I'll just come right out and say it. Are you and Ragnar an item?"

Ella's heart jolted. The frankness of the question shocked her and she didn't know where to look. "Wow, you don't beat around the bush," she tried to joke.

"Sorry, I know. But are you?" Macey stared at her intently. "I mean, you seem to be spending a lot of time together, and I've noticed that you're sharing a ride to church most Sundays."

"Well, we do live on the same road. It just seemed to make sense to carpool instead of taking two separate ones," Ella said, wondering why she felt a need to justify herself. She frowned. "Do you have some sort of a problem with that?"

Macey continued to stare at Ella as though she was trying to probe her thoughts. She was quiet for a moment then said, "This has been on my heart for a while. Since I've started, I'll just go ahead and say it, even though you say you're not involved with him. I'm really sorry if I'm off base." She took a deep breath. "I don't know whether you're aware that Zuri was my best friend. Ragnar's wife."

Ella wondered where this was going, but she felt a growing sense of unease. Macey's brown eyes were still fixed on her.

"Zuri told me a lot about her life, and that included her marriage. And I have to tell you that although she really loved Ragnar, she wasn't completely happy with their relationship."

"What?" Ella whispered. The unease was growing into dread.

Macey held up her hands. "Now, I'm not saying that he cheated on her or was abusive or anything like that. But he wasn't the most supportive of husbands. She definitely felt very much alone at times." Macey grunted in frustration.

"Goodness, I'm putting this so badly. I mean, Zuri told me she felt like she and even their child came at the bottom of his priority list. At the time they were married he was building up this business of his. This computer company that he has, the one that's made him a multi-gazillionaire. It was like he was obsessed with it twenty-four seven. He would live and breathe that company. Working really late hours, sometimes even spending the night at the office. Or at least that's where he said he was spending the night."

Macey shook her head. "Okay, maybe that bit wasn't fair of me. There was never any evidence that he wasn't where he said. But he was so fully absorbed with his work that Zuri was alone a lot. When she was pregnant with Sophie, he didn't make it for any of the appointments. There was always some urgent business issue or other to deal with. And if she hadn't had such a long labor, he might have even missed the birth. And, remember, Zuri was from Kenya, so it's not like she had loads of family to be with her. All she had was him." Macey paused for a moment and looked at Ella as though waiting for an answer.

Ella's throat was dry, and her mind was blank.

Macey went on. "And after the baby came, the same thing went on. I went to visit her the week after Sophie was born and I found her at home in floods of tears. Ragnar had to go to the office to deal with some emergency or other and he'd been gone since six o'clock that morning. This was after he'd come in after midnight the night before. Zuri was exhausted. She'd been up all night because the baby wasn't sleeping. The house was in a complete state; she couldn't remember when she'd last eaten or even had time for a shower, and Sophie was almost out of diapers. I made Zuri go to bed while I took Sophie out in her buggy and went to the corner shop to get some diapers and a few other groceries. Zuri was a very private person, but after I found her at home, that's when all of this came out in bits and pieces."

Macey sighed. "I know that some people would say that that's how it is when you're starting a business. We all know that it takes a ridiculous amount of work when you're trying to get a company off the ground. But this had been going on for months. Years. As long as I knew them Ragnar had always been like this, had this tendency to get obsessed with his work. And this was his baby for crying out loud. And his wife had no one else to lean on but him. But it just carried on. So, sorry, but I couldn't see you getting closer to him without telling you this. I have no time for a man who could treat his wife like that."

Ella's mind was in a tailspin. "Wow. That's... I don't know what to say about that. Thanks for telling me."

Macey said, "And so when I saw him hanging around you, it just made me wonder. You're a lot like Zuri, and that's clearly what he likes in his women. Really sweet, gentle, compliant and, no offense, but you let people walk all over you. And you don't have much family support either. I don't want anyone taking advantage of you, and I thought I'd seen a pattern."

Ella nodded mechanically, too stunned to be offended by her friend's assessment of her.

Macey's lips twisted in a humorless smile. "You probably already got a vibe that I'm not Ragnar Klassen's number one fan. Well, now you know why." She slapped the table with both hands and pushed her chair back. "I've said my piece. Sorry if I'm sticking my nose in, but this was really heavy on my heart and I thought it was important that you know. Still friends?"

Ella managed a smile. "Yes, of course. I really appreciate you telling me this."

Macey leaned over and hugged her. "You're way too good for a guy like that, hun. You know that, right? You deserve someone who'll treat you like a princess. Don't settle for anything less. Okay, I'm going to try to catch the tail end of the class. You coming?"

Ella shook her head. "No, I'll just sit here for a minute." Macey nodded and hugged her again, then left the room. Ella rubbed her temples. What was she supposed to do with all this? In the days after she'd met with Ragnar's siblings, he hadn't said anything, but she'd begun to think more and more about what it would be like to be a real family.

She'd been observing him more closely, and his good qualities seemed so clear and were growing on her. He was attentive, helpful, and considerate. His daughter clearly adored him, and Tiffany did, too. From all that she had seen, he was a devoted father, closely in tune with Sophie's needs. But Macey had been Zuri's best friend. She'd had ringside seats to Ragnar's relationship with his wife. Ella couldn't just discount what Macey had observed.

She thought back to how Macey had been one of her first friends when she had started coming to Immanuel. She had immediately been drawn to Macey's warm candid personality. That was why Macey's coldness to Ragnar had surprised her. Macey was chatty and friendly with everyone but barely had anything to say to him.

Most of all, Ella was struck by Macey's story of Zuri alone with her new baby and low on groceries. She could remember being that new mother on her own. Except in her case Neil had been out partying, not working. She shuddered, remembering the isolation and deep sadness of those days. But Ragnar wasn't like that, was he?

Her eyes flew up to the clock on the wall. It was almost time to pick up Tiffany from her class.

Ella met Ragnar standing outside their daughters' Sunday school class along with a couple of other parents. She avoided his eyes as they all made the usual Sunday morning surface-level chitchat at the pre-service coffee and fellowship time.

She sat next to him during the service, as was usual these days, while their daughters kept themselves quietly occupied with a generous supply of felt tip pens, coloring books, and stickers. Ella barely heard what was going on as she turned Macey's words over and over in her mind.

She threw several sidelong glances at Ragnar as the service went on, watching his profile as he sang the hymns and bowed his head in prayer. He seemed to be everything that

Neil was not. Neil was all about the flashy exterior, and that had been enough to beguile and win her. But it was Ragnar's deeper qualities that were making inroads into her heart. His kindness, his sense of humor, his generosity. The Ragnar she was getting to know was nothing like the one Macey had described. He made her feel safe and beautiful. That couldn't all be an act.

As she defended him in her mind and resisted Macey's low opinion of him, she realized that her heart was more than halfway gone. She wanted Macey to be wrong because she was beginning to fall in love with Ragnar.

Chapter Nineteen

ELLA WAS QUIETER than usual as Ragnar drove her and the girls home from the service. The children were eager to watch some videos together, so he set them up in Sophie's room with the latest season of *My Little Pony*. He hoped that would keep them busy for a while, because he wanted to speak to Ella with no interruptions.

He went back downstairs to the conservatory. Ella was looking out at the back yard, her back toward him. Sunshine filled the room and bathed her in a warm glow. He had been rehearsing what to say for many days, but his mouth felt dry as he looked at her, framed against the backdrop of the garden. He might be about to shatter their friendship, but it was a risk worth taking. Still, he wanted to prolong the moment and remember her like this, just in case it all went wrong.

She must have heard his intake of breath because she turned around. He stepped into the room and closed the door behind him. "They're busy upstairs."

"Maybe I should pop over to my house and get a few things done," she said, moving to the sofa where she had left her purse.

She was leaving. Another chance was slipping away. But he couldn't let her go. He wanted to find out today. Right now.

He moved forward. "Ella, can we talk for a minute?"

She looked up at him and he plunged ahead. "Please sit down." He gestured toward the sofa, and she sat down on the edge, clutching her purse.

"We've been friends for a while. And it's been such a blessing for Sophie and for me to get to know you." She looked down at her hands. Ragnar swallowed. "Our lives have been so much better since we met you. And it's not just because you're so amazing with Sophie. I feel a connection with you, and I want to explore it further. I want to be more than friends. I don't even know if you're interested in a relationship with anyone, let alone me, but that's what I want with you. If you don't want that, then I'll just shut up."

She looked up at him and he was surprised to see that her eyes were moist. "I... I enjoy spending time with you, and I like you as a friend. But I'm afraid—"

She looked past his shoulder at the door, just as he heard footsteps approaching. He turned around to see Sophie heading toward them. She pushed open the glass door.

"Dad, the episode's frozen. It got stuck and we don't know how to start it again."

"Okay, let's see what's going on," Ragnar said. Of all the times for the blasted thing to have a glitch. His heart racing, he fought back his impatience and followed Sophie back to her room. He rebooted the streaming service, which, thankfully, was functioning well again. He came back downstairs, desperate to carry on his talk with Ella.

She was still on the sofa, head bowed, her hands balled into fists on her lap.

"Sorry about that," he said. "I got the video to work again. What were you saying?"

He could see the sheen of tears in her brown eyes, and his anxiety spiked. She was going to turn him down.

She said, "I'm really flattered by what you said about me. I really like you, and so does Tiffany. I can see us being more than just friends, and I would like that." She looked down at her hands. "But I've got things badly wrong before, and I don't want to rush into anything. We've both been married before, and we've got the girls to think about. I don't want to make a mistake. I don't want you to make a mistake, either." Her eyes met his again.

He moved over to the armchair in front of her. "We could take things as slowly as you need to. We can take all the time we want." He reached out and took her hands in his. "I just wanted to make it clear that I feel a lot more for you than just friendship, because it's getting kind of hard to hide."

She smiled for the first time and he asked, "So, are we dating, then?"

"I guess we are," she said.

Heart bounding, he sat next to her and drew her into his arms. How he'd longed to do that! He breathed in deep, the scent of her, the feel of her, making his senses dizzy. He bent his head down and kissed her lips, his touch feather-light. She stiffened and for a moment it felt like he was kissing a sculpture made of ice. He was about to draw back when her lips softened, her arms curled round him, and he knew that this wasn't an unfeeling statue. She was a warm, living woman. He kissed her again and tightened his embrace, drawing in a long breath.

"Wow," he said. His pulse was racing, and every sense was alive to her presence. The weight of her head on his shoulder, the delicate fragrance of her lavender perfume, her shapely hand resting on his arm. He drew a long, shaky breath. "I'm sorry, that wasn't exactly taking things slow."

She chuckled. "No, not quite."

He picked up her hand, twining his fingers with hers. "What shall we tell the girls?"

"I don't know. I'm not sure how Tiffany will take it, to be honest. Shall we just keep things quiet for a while? Take it really slow and play it by ear?"

He nodded. These were unchartered waters. His heart was soaring with the knowledge that this beautiful woman with such a kind and gentle spirit was attracted to him, but he could see that the way ahead was far from straightforward. Taking things slow felt wise. The last thing he wanted to do was steam ahead and crash on an iceberg. He rested his cheek on her hair.

Ella and Tiffany left soon after dinner, a slow-cooked beef stew which Ragnar served with crusty bread and brown rice. His phone rang while Sophie was brushing her teeth. Seeing it was his brother Magnus, he pushed open the French doors and stepped out into the garden.

"Hey," he said. "What's up?"

"Hi," Magnus said. "How's your Sunday?"

"Fantastic, actually," Ragnar said. "Ella and I are officially a couple. As of this afternoon."

"Wow, that's awesome! Hang on a minute," Magnus said. His voice was muffled, and Ragnar heard him call out, "Hey, Nia, Ragnar's dating Ella. Yeah, I will." His voice became clear again. "Nia says she approves, and congratulations."

"Thanks!" Ragnar said. "We haven't told the girls yet. We'll just take things really slow for now. Maybe even talk to our pastor, see about getting couples counseling since we're not exactly fresh young things like you and your lovely wife."

"That sounds wise," Magnus said. "I'm really happy for you. Nia and I have been praying for you, and I think she'll be good for you. I'm guessing you're not going to tell Mother and Father just yet?"

"You're guessing right," Ragnar said. He operated on a need-to-know basis with his parents, and they did not need to know that he was in a new relationship. To her credit, his mother hadn't minded him marrying a penniless African student. Jessica Klassen was all about appearances and Zuri, who had borne a striking resemblance to the supermodel Iman, had won her approval on sight. Ella didn't have the same classical beauty as Zuri, but she was lovely, and he knew his mother would endorse her based on that. His father was a different story, however. He'd been cynical and abrasive with Zuri, but that's how he was with everybody.

In many ways, Ragnar had always been the black sheep of the family, breaking out of the mold early on and forging his own path. Although he was the eldest son, he had turned down the chance to have a role in any of his father's business enterprises. So, when he broke with convention even further and chose a bride who was not only outside the family's social circle but from a different race, it was yet another act of a young man known for doing his own thing.

He didn't want to expose Ella and Tiffany to his parents until their relationship was on a more solid footing. No, informing Karl and Jessica would have to wait.

"I'll tell Vanya, though, of course," Ragnar continued. "I hope they'll be friends."

"Awesome," Magnus said. "We should get together soon. I'll ask Nia when we can have you all over to visit."

"Sounds great," Ragnar said.

Magnus said, "In all this excitement, I almost forgot. I'd called to talk to you about something else, but your news had driven it clean out of my head."

"Oh? What?"

"Remember that afternoon when we kind of soft-balled the idea of working together?"

"Yes, the biologics discovery idea," Ragnar said.

"That's it," Magnus said. "Well, I think Nordic Wind is going to go ahead with this. Acricaine is doing well, but we don't want to rest on our laurels. We need to build on what we have."

Ragnar nodded, although his brother couldn't see him. Magnus's pharmaceutical company, Nordic Wind, owned a groundbreaking HIV/AIDS medicine that was changing the treatment landscape. It was giving Magnus more success than he had ever dreamed possible, but Ragnar knew that Magnus was even more thankful for how his work with the medicine had brought him and Nia together, and for how many lives it was saving across the world.

"So, you want me involved?" Ragnar asked.

"If you're interested," Magnus said. "You're going to have all this time on your hands once you're done with your handover. Would you be able to meet up with Alex and me to talk about it more?"

Alex was Magnus's business partner in Nordic Wind and the brains behind Acricaine. She preferred to focus on pharmaceutical development while Magnus handled the business side of things. "Okay," Ragnar said. "Have your people call my people. Just kidding," he laughed. "I have no people. Let me know when you want to meet, and we'll take it from there."

"Excellent. Talk to you soon," Magnus said, and hung up.

Ragnar smiled. He didn't know the details of what Magnus had in mind, but he already liked the sound of it. He breathed a prayer of thanks. Ella was going to be by his side, and he had a possible new business opportunity with his brother. Life was looking good.

Chapter Twenty

A FEW DAYS later, Ella and Ragnar stood side by side in his living room, Sophie perched on a stool in front of them. The child had a towel wrapped around her, and her damp curls were spread over her shoulders.

"Okay," Ragnar said. "We've washed and conditioned the hair. It's not dripping wet but not completely dry either. What do I do next?"

Ella held up a spray bottle. "I've filled this up with water, conditioner, and hair oil. Moisture is a curly head's best friend. Curls are very thirsty, especially if the hair is of African origin. So, you always need to spray some of this on when you're doing anything with her hair. Don't touch her hair unless you moisten it first."

"Oh yeah, that's right," Ragnar said. "Everyone in those curly hair care YouTube videos has those bottles."

"Good, you've been paying attention, my young padawan," Ella said. "Do you remember what else you need?"

Ragnar looked at the array of hair implements laid out on the table next to him. "Um, wide-toothed comb?"

"Excellent! What else?"

Ragnar scratched his head and Ella laughed at his puzzlement. "Tangle Teazer brush," she said, holding up a small plastic hairbrush with soft flexible bristles. "So, give her hair a squirt from the spray bottle."

Ragnar obeyed. Ella said, "Then brush through it." She watched as Ragnar pulled the brush through the child's hair.

"Ow!" Sophie said.

"You need to start from the tips," Ella said, "like this." She took the brush from Ragnar and demonstrated how to de-tangle Sophie's wet curls, starting from the tips and working upward to the roots of her hair. "Are you okay Sophie?"

"Yeah, I'm fine," the child said. "You do it much better than Dad does."

"Dad's got to learn too," Ella said, "and I think he's doing a great job. YouTube is a fantastic teacher."

"You're a fantastic teacher," Ragnar said, snaking an arm around her waist and giving her a squeeze. He nuzzled her neck and she elbowed him gently in the ribs, pointing at

Sophie. They had not yet told the girls about their relationship, and much as she loved his displays of affection, she did not want the children to see just yet.

Ragnar winked at her and carried on brushing his daughter's hair with slow, gentle strokes.

"Much better," Ella said. "What do you think, Sophie?"

"It doesn't hurt," Sophie said.

"Your hair looks really nice," Tiffany said, looking up from her tablet. "Are you going to make it like this?" She pointed at a picture of a young mixed race girl whose hair was twisted in Bantu knots.

"I like those," Sophie said. "Can you do my hair like that, Dad?"

Ragnar laughed. "I can barely brush it correctly. Apparently, I've been doing it wrong all this time. We'll see how far I get with Ella helping."

"Those do look cute," Ella said. "Let's get the hair brushed first." Ragnar finished one section and started on the next. A loud ring tone filled the air.

"That's my phone," Ragnar said. "Could you grab that please, Tiffany? It's on the coffee table."

Tiffany picked up his phone and handed it to him. He glanced at the caller ID. "I have to take this," he said, pushing the answer button and handing the hairbrush to Ella. "Hello? Hi, Dave." He walked toward the kitchen.

Ella waited a few minutes, but Ragnar continued his conversation, heading out the French doors and onto the deck. She smiled as she watched him step outside. Being here with him and the girls, doing regular family things felt anything but humdrum. It felt natural. Safe. Restful. It was exactly what she wanted and needed. Neil had always reminded her of a caged tiger when they were at home. Family time bored him, and tension and irritation rolled off him in waves that had set her and Tiffany on edge. The last thing Neil would have done was spend an afternoon learning how to care for his daughter's hair.

She squirted more liquid onto Sophie's curls. She could complete the de-tangling and then, when he was done with his call, show Ragnar how to divide the hair into sections for plaiting.

He came back in, frowning. He looked at Ella. "That was Dave. They're having a huge problem with their software roll-out to their new banking client. I'll have to go in and help them."

"Today?" she said. "But it's Saturday."

"I know, and they wouldn't have called me unless things were tight.

I'm sorry. Would you mind taking care of Sophie until I get back?"

"No, of course not," Ella said. "We'll be fine, won't we?" The girls nodded.

"Thanks," Ragnar said. He went to the kitchen sink and turned on the tap, washing the hair products off his hands. "I told them that they still needed to do some more testing under different conditions, and it was a bit too early to start the full roll-out, but they wanted to do it this weekend. I designed the code, so I need to help them figure out what's gone wrong." He dried his hands and looked at his shirt, which was damp from the shampooing session with Sophie. "I'd better change out of this," he said.

"Let's just get your hair done, shall we?" Ella said to Sophie. "Bantu knots, was it?" She began to part the hair into sections.

Ragnar came back into the living room, fastening the last button on a fresh shirt. He grabbed his wallet and keys from the counter and put them in his pocket. He stepped up to Sophie. "Bye, sweetheart. See you soon." He kissed her forehead, and stroked Ella gently on her back. She knew that would have to stand in for a goodbye kiss. "I'm not sure how long it'll take to fix this," he said. "I'll give you a call as soon as I figure out how long they'll need me."

Ella nodded and he walked out the door.

She didn't hear from him until several hours later, when she was wondering whether or not to hold dinner for him. He called her on her cell phone. "I'm so sorry, Ella. It's full panic stations here. The bank's clients can't access their accounts or use their debit cards. I think we figured out what's causing this, but we're having to roll back to a previous version of the software, and it might take a while to sort it all out."

"Sounds hectic," Ella said. "But thank God you know how to fix it."

"Yes," he said, "thank God indeed. This is Theta Software's biggest client and I'd hate for things to go wrong just before I leave the company. I might be late getting back. Would you mind having Sophie stay over with you just in case?"

"No, that should be fine."

"Thank you," he said. "Could I just have a quick word with her?"

"Of course," Ella said. She crossed to the foot of the stairs and called up. "Sophie, your dad's on the phone."

Sophie came down the stairs and grabbed the phone. "Hi, Dad. Uh huh." She listened for a moment then said, "Okay. Love you too,

Dad. Bye." She gave the phone back to Ella and went back upstairs to join Tiffany.

Ella pressed the phone back onto her ear. "Hello, Ragnar?"

"Hi. She's fine with it," he said. "Thank you so much. I'd better get back to work."

"Should I keep some dinner for you?"

"No, you don't need to," he said. "I've already asked you to do enough. Thanks, once again. See you later."

"Bye," she said, but he'd already hung up.

Chapter Twenty-One

ATER THAT EVENING as the girls' bedtime approached and Ragnar still hadn't returned, Ella took Tiffany and Sophie back to her house. Jocelyn and Jarvis were due to stop by to say goodbye before they left for their extended stay in the Greek islands the next morning.

When they came through the front door, Jocelyn's eyes went wide at the sight of Sophie in her pajamas alongside her own granddaughter.

"Sophie's dad is working late to-night, so she's staying over," Ella said.

"You're doing your child-minding work on a Saturday night?" Jocelyn asked. "That's what I call dedication."

Jocelyn chatted with the girls for a few minutes and read them a story until it was time for them to go to bed. Ella went to tuck them in while Jocelyn and Jarvis sat in the living room with cups of coffee.

Ella came back in and sat in an armchair across from them. "I might as well tell you, although not many people know, and we're still keeping it quiet from the girls." She took a deep breath. "Sophie's dad and I are dating."

Jocelyn's hands flew up to cover her mouth. "Oh! I see." She fanned her face with her fluttering hands, and tears filled her eyes. She jumped up. "I'm sorry. Just give me a moment." She stumbled toward the back door and walked out into the garden.

Jarvis followed his partner with his eyes. Ella thought he would go out and comfort Jocelyn, but instead he turned his gaze back to Ella, a smile spreading across his face. "Well, well, well." His hard eyes glittered. "Congratulations to him, and to you, of course. Not bad. Not bad at all." He raised his coffee cup in mock salute. "An excellent maneuver. He's worth a fair bit, so you'll be sitting pretty. And I can't blame him for his choice, of course."

His smile turned into a leer. "He'll be getting a delicious and succulent pound or two of flesh out of the deal. I've always been partial to dark chocolate and black coffee myself. You know what they say. The darker the berry the sweeter the juice. You girls know how to handle your business in the sack." He ran his tongue over the rim of his cup.

Ella glared at him, her fists clenched, nails digging into her palms. White hot rage seared through her body. "That's enough," she hissed. "You're disgusting."

"Oh, come on now," he said. "You're no blushing virgin. I'm just complimenting you on playing your cards so well, using your abundant charms to such devastating effect. Here I was, almost getting offended that I couldn't get a look in, not knowing that you were busy angling for a much bigger fish with deeper pockets. Well played, Ella." He raised his cup again.

Hot tears stinging her eyes, she stood up and went to the kitchen before she could act on her impulse to tip the mug of scalding coffee over his head.

Jocelyn came back in, face blotchy, eyes damp. She saw Ella and came over to her. "I'm so sorry, sweetheart," she said, holding a tissue to her eyes. "This just took me by surprise. I wasn't expecting that, and I was just thinking of poor Neil. But of course this was bound to happen. You're still young and beautiful, and I should have known this day would come. I just didn't know it would be so soon."

Her voice trembled and Ella thought she was about to break down again. But Jocelyn drew in a deep breath and said, "I wish you well, darling. I wish you all the happiness you deserve." She hugged Ella. "I just hope he'll be good to my little Tiffany. You know, his having a child already and all that. And his daughter will be entitled to so much more, being a blood relative of the Klassens and all, and I just don't want Tiffany to feel like a poor relation since she'll be his stepchild. But I'm sure you thought through all of this."

Jocelyn's words stabbed deep, but Ella forced a smile. "Thanks, Jocelyn. He's been very kind to Tiffany."

"Does his family know about this?" Jocelyn asked.

"A few of them," Ella said. "We're taking it slow and, like I said, we haven't even told the girls yet. So, please keep it to yourselves for now. I just didn't want you finding out from somewhere else."

Ella was already regretting telling them. They were going away tomorrow. Why hadn't she just kept her mouth shut?

"I appreciate that, sweetheart," Jocelyn said, giving Ella another hug. "Don't mind me, I'm just being silly." Her eyes filled with tears again. "All right. We'd best be on our way now. Give Tiffany a big hug from me when she gets up."

Jarvis stood up, his eyes fixed on Ella.

"Have a lovely time, Jocelyn," Ella said. She refused to look at Jarvis, relieved that she would be spared the sight of him for a few months. She followed them to the door and closed it behind them.

Chapter Twenty-Two

ELLA GATHERED UP the post-lunch detritus from her picnic blanket. She loved the church's annual midsummer picnic which was traditionally held at Hatbrook Memorial Park. The church members sat scattered across the soft grass, making the most of the day. A bank of white clouds kept them from the full glare of the sun, but there was no threat of rain.

The older children had been pulled together into a game of cricket while the younger ones, Tiffany and Sophie among them, played in a large sandpit.

Ella placed the trash inside a bag, ready to take it to the nearest recycling bins. She caught sight of Ragnar approaching, looking relaxed in tan shorts and a T-shirt. "I'll get rid of that for you," he said, taking the trash. "I've just caught up with Pastor Jonathan. He's got a spare moment to talk to us if you're okay to do that now. Can you come?"

"Okay, sure," Ella said. She and Ragnar had talked about approaching their pastor for couple's counseling. She hadn't expected to have a chat with him out here in front of everyone, though. She stood up and brushed the crumbs off her denim skirt and followed Ragnar, conscious of the gaze of several church members who watched them as they walked to the edge of the impromptu cricket oval.

They hadn't told anyone yet about their relationship, but she knew that people weren't blind.

Pastor Jonathan Gary, in his 60s, was a tall thin man with wispy hair and a kind and earnest face. He saw Ella and Ragnar coming and smiled. "Hello, Ella," he said. "Ragnar says you'd like to have a word." They walked a short distance away from the group of cricket players and the other adults who were supervising the game.

"Thank you so much for your time, Pastor Jonathan," Ragnar said. His hand found Ella's and gave it a squeeze. "Ella and I have been getting to know each other for a while, since Sophie I came back and found that she and Tiffany moved into my neighborhood. The girls are really good friends, and we've grown closer as well." He looked at Ella and smiled. "We've recently decided that we want to enter into a relationship."

Pastor Jonathan's eyebrows flew up and his face brightened. Ella turned her eyes to the ground.

Ragnar went on. "Because of our situation, both of us having lost our spouses and being parents of young children, we want to build as strong a foundation as possible, and we thought it would be wise to come to you early on and seek your help and advice as we go forward with this. Would that be possible?"

Pastor Jonathan beamed. "First of all, congratulations! I have known you both for a while, and I know you both love the Lord. I'm delighted that you found each other and even more delighted that you're seeking to go forward with wisdom. It's definitely a wise choice to get some sort of counseling or at least talk through things with a third party, given all that you have both been through over the last two years. I'm flattered that you've come to me for that and I will do my best. Have you told your daughters?" He looked back and forth between them.

"No, not yet," Ella said. "We thought it best to wait a while."

"Not a bad idea," said Pastor Jonathan. "You need to tread a fine line, telling them when you're ready, but not letting them find out from somebody else and be the last to know. On the other hand, you'd be surprised how much they may have picked up already. Children are a lot more observant than we give them credit for. But these are some of the things we will explore when we talk. How soon do you want to meet?"

Ragnar glanced at Ella. "Next week?" Ella nodded.

"That will be fine. Just call the church secretary and she'll set up the appointment," Pastor Jonathan said. He smiled again. "I am really happy for the two of you and will definitely keep you and your girls in prayer." He wrung Ragnar's hand and patted his shoulder, then turned and shook Ella's hand as well. "I'd better get back to watching this cricket match," he said. "I'm supposed to hand out the prizes."

"All right, Pastor Jonathan," Ragnar said. "Thank you so much for your time, and we'll speak to you soon."

His hand rested on the small of Ella's back as they turned and headed back to their picnic blankets. Ella caught sight of Macey Travis sitting on the grass, her eyes fixed on them. Cold fingers of apprehension gripped her stomach. "Go on ahead," she said to Ragnar. "I just need to speak to someone. See you in a minute."

She took a deep breath and walked toward Macey. She had not spoken much with her friend since their conversation that other Sunday when Macey had tried to warn her away from Ragnar. She hadn't consciously been avoiding her, but this was not a conversation she was eager to have. Ella squirmed inside. She wondered how Macey would react when she told her that she had started dating Ragnar immediately after that warning.

Ella came up to Macey and knelt down at the edge of the picnic blanket, hoping her smile didn't look as fake as it felt. "Hi. It's been a while."

"Yes, it has," Macey said, tucking a brown curl under her straw hat. "How have you been?"

"Fine," Ella said. "You?"

"Oh, fine. Nothing to tell."

"Um, you probably saw us speaking with Pastor Jonathan just now,"

Ella said, forcing herself to look into Macey's eyes.

"I did. I'm guessing you're going to tell me what that was about."

Ella nodded and held her gaze. "Ragnar and I are dating."

The shadow of a smile twisted Macey's mouth. "I figured out as much. I could see it coming. That must work out very nicely for him. Dating his childminder means he gets even more freedom to work longer and longer hours. Tell me, has he started leaving her with you beyond normal working hours yet?"

Heat rushed to Ella's face and her mouth dropped open.

Macey nodded, her lips compressed together. "Of course he has. Didn't take him long at all to start taking advantage of you."

"It's not like that," Ella said. "He needed a favor and I was happy to help. I'm sorry that you can't be happy for us." She started to get up.

Macey held up a hand. "I'm sorry; that was out of line. Listen, Ella, let's not feel all weird about this. You know what I think about Ragnar, but of course you're a grown woman and you're smart enough to make your own decisions. And in any case, I knew him a while ago; perhaps he's changed after all he's been through. I would love to be wrong. Anyway, I wish you all the best. I really do." She reached out and gave Ella a quick hug.

"Thank you," Ella said. "I really appreciate that."

"So, when did all this happen?" Macey asked.

"It's been a few weeks," Ella said. Her friend nodded and changed the subject. They chatted briefly about neutral topics until the words petered out. Ella had the sense that neither of them was saying what was uppermost in their minds: her new relationship with Ragnar.

She stood up. "I'd better get back. Tiffany will be coming back soon, desperate for a drink or the bathroom or both."

Macey smiled. "Okay, then. Speak to you soon."

Ella walked back toward Ragnar. She wondered how long this barrier of awkwardness would last between her and her friend.

Chapter Twenty-Three

ELLA CAME BACK downstairs after checking on the girls, who were lying fast asleep in Sophie's room. "They're completely dead to the world," she said to Ragnar and his sister Vanya, who were sitting in the living room. "I believe the plan worked."

"The plan" had been to thoroughly tire the girls out so they would fall asleep early, leaving their parents free to go on their first date alone. Ella had taken the girls swimming, and then on a long tramp through the countryside, and while she made their dinner, they had tried out Sophie's new trampoline. Both children had been so exhausted that Sophie had begun to doze off over her dinner plate, and when they went to bed, both of them were asleep within five minutes.

"Excellent," Vanya said. She had come to stay in the house while Ella and Ragnar went out. "I'll take it from here; you guys go get yourselves ready."

"Thank you," Ella said. "I'll just head over to my place."

"Pick you up in half an hour?" Ragnar asked.

"Make it forty-five minutes," Ella said. She'd not had the chance to dress up for Ragnar before, and she hoped the outfit she'd chosen would hit the mark. It was a floor-length peasant-style evening dress with a wide neckline that exposed the tops of her shoulders and a fabric belt that cinched in her middle, showing off her still-slender waist. She had not worn it for years but found, thankfully, that it still just about fit.

She took a lightning fast shower and then engaged a quick debate over what sort of make-up to wear. Neil liked it best when she went for full-on glamor, complete with heavy foundation, smoky eyes, false eyelashes, and bright lipstick. But she didn't have the time to get completely dolled up. Even more, she didn't want to. Wearing her full-coverage makeup had always felt too much like putting on the perfect mask she'd displayed to the world when she was breaking inside. No, she wouldn't be doing that tonight. But she did need to freshen up her face. She finally decided on a tinted moisturizer, mascara, eyeliner, and clear lip gloss.

She was just spritzing up her short curls when Ragnar knocked on the door, right on the dot. She let him in and the look on his face told that her efforts had not been in vain. "You look stunning," he said, taking her in from head to foot.

The way his eyes drank her in made her stomach flutter. The feeling was a world away from the crawling disgust she felt under Jarvis's gaze.

"Thank you," she said. "You don't look too bad yourself." Ragnar wore a dinner jacket over an evening shirt with no tie, and dark tan slacks.

"I'll just grab my shoes," she said, slipping her feet into a pair of high-heeled mules.

"Your carriage awaits, Cinderella," Ragnar said. They were going in his car, which stood parked in front of her house. He opened the door for her, and she stepped in and buckled up as he shut the door and went around to the driver's side.

"I have no intention of losing a shoe at midnight," Ella said.

Ragnar laughed as he started up the engine.

"So, where are we going?" she asked as he eased out of the driveway.

"A little place called the Grange Inn."

Ella could vaguely remember hearing the name, possibly in one of Jocelyn's glossy magazines. She settled back into the soft leather upholstery as Ragnar steered the car out onto the dual carriageway. She felt like a teenager going on her first date. Ever since Ragnar and she had become a couple, they had continued to see a lot of each other, but always with the girls present. The only chances they'd been able to snatch time alone was on the few occasions when the girls had a sleepover and they'd been able to sit up in the living room while the children slept.

Ella was grateful for Vanya's willingness to stay over and make this evening out possible.

Sooner than she'd expected, Ragnar turned off the dual carriageway and began driving on narrow country roads that Ella had not seen before. In about ten minutes they arrived at a secluded country estate, which a modest but well-lit sign proclaimed to be the Grange Inn. Ragnar found a spot in the parking lot and walked around to let Ella out of the car.

Her eyes took in the surroundings. The Grange Inn was a sprawling Elizabethan-era stone building with ivy climbing up its walls. Ragnar laced his fingers with hers as they walked up to the entrance. A Maître d' welcomed them, inclining his head as Ragnar said his name.

"Welcome, Mr. Klassen and madam," he said. "Your table is ready. Please come this way."

He led them to a private dining room where a candlelit table was set for two. Ella eased into her chair. Wait staff presented drinks menus and faded discreetly into the background.

"This place is beautiful," Ella said. She was about to ask him whether he'd been here before, then stopped herself. If he had come here, it had probably been with his wife. She pushed the thought away, determined to enjoy the moment with no ghosts from the past.

They ordered their meal and when they were alone, Ragnar reached across the table to hold Ella's hand. He stroked her fingers, and she was surprised at the sparks of electricity that simple motion set off. She swallowed a sip of water, hoping that would settle her nerves.

"Did you have a good day today at work? All disaster averted?" She cringed at her questions, but her mind had gone blank. Alone with him for the first time, his thumb tracing small circles on the back of her hand, his eyes looking at her that way, she felt vulnerable and exposed.

"All is going well," he said. "I hope the transition will be smooth from now on until Theta Software is out of my hands. Actually, I wanted to talk to you a bit about that." His expression changed, a boy-like eagerness lighting up his eyes. "I think I told you that I've been wondering and praying about what to do once I finally leave Theta. As it turns out, Magnus and I might go into business together."

"Really? That sounds great."

"I know," he said with a grin. She listened to the excitement in his voice as he told her about how

Nordic Wind, Magnus's pharma company, was expanding its biologics development department and needed somebody with a strong IT background to head it up. After explaining what the department would do, he said, "Magnus and I think this could be an exciting opportunity to explore. And I think it will be awesome to work with him. He's my best friend as well as my brother. So, we will be putting our heads together along with Vanya and Magnus's business partner Alex to work out the details."

"Wow," Ella said. "The timing seems to have worked out perfectly for you."

"Yes, it's amazing," he said. "It does overlap with what would have been a busy time anyway as I finish up with Theta. But Magnus and his people are ready to move forward with this." He looked at her intently. "It will mean I'll have some long days at work over the next few weeks. But I hope things will settle down soon."

Faint alarm bells sounded in the back of her mind, but she pushed them firmly away. "I really am happy for you."

"For us," he said, covering her hand with his, his tone making her insides feel like jelly.

The servers brought their entrées and they turned their attention to the delicious food set before them. Ella's steak practically melted in her mouth and her vegetables tasted almost too good to have been grown in anything so earthly as dirt.

As they ate, Ragnar filled Ella in on more details about his new business venture. His enthusiasm was infectious and she was happy to see him so excited.

When they finished, a waiter asked whether he could offer them a dessert menu. Ragnar looked at Ella. "I'm stuffed," she said.

Ragnar said to the waiter, "Me too. Perhaps we could look at it a bit later?"

"Of course, sir," the waiter said. "If I might be so bold as to recommend it, the gardens are particularly beautiful tonight. They are always spectacular at night, and the moon is out this evening."

"Thank you," Ragnar said. "I quite like the sound of that." He turned to Ella. "What do you think? A little moonlit stroll before dessert?"

"Sounds good," she said.

The dining room opened onto a terrace, which led on into the landscaped garden. Fairy lights were strung around the shrubbery, and the full moon flooded the scenery with a silvery light.

When they stepped outside, Ella shivered. The evening air was cooler than she had expected. She was about to suggest going back in to get her wrap, but Ragnar slipped off his jacket and draped it around her shoulders, encircling her with his arm. His tantalizing scent of ambergris and patchouli surrounded her as they walked slowly along the garden path.

They stopped in front of a fountain with stonework carved in the shape of a mermaid. Ragnar steered her over to a stone bench. They sat down and he pulled her closer. She leaned into him, giving herself over to the moment. She felt him shifting his position, and the warm gentle pressure of his lips as he kissed her.

Her mind wheeled, wanting him to continue, yet frightened that he would. As though sensing her hesitation, he sat back, keeping his arm around her. She was relieved. Her heart thumped so hard that she could hear it in her ears. She loved being close to him, but although his kisses delighted her, they also brought about a rising sense of panic that she could not understand, and that in itself scared her.

"Are you okay?" he asked softly.

She nodded. "Yes, I'm fine."

They sat in silence for a moment. She couldn't make sense of her own confused and broken thoughts. She loved this man, and she could sense that he had strong feelings for her as well. Tonight in this exquisite place, this should have been the perfect moment to relax and just let the magic work. But as she grew closer to him, she felt tendrils of fear tighten their grip inside her. It was like diving into a deep pool, exhilarating at first, then she began getting desperate for air and didn't know which way the surface was.

"It's beautiful here, isn't it?" he asked.

"Yes," she said, glad for the banal question that helped her focus her mind. "It's amazing. How did you find out about it?"

His answer was so long in coming that she thought he hadn't heard her. "I came here a long time ago with my wife."

He hesitated for a moment then said, "I'm sorry. Maybe I shouldn't have—"

"No apology needed," Ella said quickly. "Of course we'll go to places that we've been to before. There's nothing wrong with that."

He answered by squeezing her shoulders tightly.

"How long were you married?" she asked.

"Five years," he said. "We met at university. We were both active in the Christian Union. Well, she was more active than I was to begin with. I just started going because it was the only way I could see her." Ella could hear the smile in his voice. "But it didn't take me long to get serious about my faith as well. We were married before graduation."

Ella didn't know what to say. She was trying to think of a comment when he asked, "How about you and Neil? How long were you married?"

"Six years," Ella said. She hoped he wouldn't ask her any more about Neil. She thought she had reached a place of calm now, where thinking about him didn't hurt anymore. But since she'd started opening her heart to Ragnar, she realized that her emotions and memories about Neil simmered constantly beneath the surface. Getting closer to Ragnar stirred up the deeper places of her heart, the place with feelings she hadn't allowed to run free since she'd given her love to Neil.

She could still remember her intense love for her husband and how it had been battered and smothered by years of bitter disappointment, neglect, and betrayal. She didn't want to talk or think about Neil.

"Ella," Ragnar said, straightening up and facing her, "I want you to understand this. Zuri is... Zuri was my past. But you are my present." He cupped her cheek with his hand. "And I want you to be my future. I know it's complicated, but I hope we can try."

Her throat constricted and she couldn't speak. She looked into his gray eyes and nodded, leaning against him as he held her. She loved him for his kindness in reassuring her about Zuri, knowing it was because he wanted to make her feel secure. But it wasn't the thought of Zuri making her tense up in his embrace. It was her memories of Neil.

Chapter Twenty-Four

"HEY, IT'S ALMOST midnight," Magnus said. He raked both hands through his hair and looked at Ragnar.

"Is it?" Ragnar checked his watch. "I can't believe it." He stood up, stretching the kinks out of his muscles.

They were in the conference room of Nordic Wind, Magnus's company. It had been a long day of brainstorming with Magnus, Vanya, and Alex. The result of their day's work was the skeleton of a business plan for Nordic Wind's expansion into biologics development. In the early evening, Alex had gone home to her young family, while Vanya had called it a day a couple of hours ago. Magnus and Ragnar had remained, working out what needed to be done next and delegating tasks.

Magnus said, "Nia knew I'd be late tonight. I hope she hasn't waited up for me; she hasn't been sleeping well lately."

Ragnar looked up, concerned. "Is the pregnancy going okay?"

"She's fine, and the baby is fine," Magnus said. "She's just exhausted, but the doctor says that's normal." He looked at his brother. "I had no idea how I thought this would be. I mean, I'm excited and happy, but most of all, I'm scared witless."

Ragnar smiled. "That's normal, too. I was scared about everything. Zuri, the baby, what kind of dad I would be, whether I'd be able to provide for them." He paused for a moment, then asked, "Did you know about my financial trouble when Zuri and I got married?"

"What financial trouble?" Magnus asked.

"You were away at St. Andrews at the time, weren't you? Well, Father responded to my engagement by cutting off my access to my trust fund. In his twisted logic, he was sure that Zuri saw marrying a Klassen as a way of latching on to the family fortune, and he decided to turn off the money tap."

"What?"

"Yup," Ragnar said. "I was pretty broke when we got married. I'd assumed that I would have money to buy a home and get off to a good start. But I had to start with nothing. You know, the way ninety-nine percent of people do. Zuri and I both worked while I tried to establish Theta Software. And then

Father came around and said I could have the money after all. I think Mother and Grandma put pressure on him. But I was a stubborn hothead and refused to take it."

Magnus shook his head. "Just when I thought I knew all the stunts Father could pull. I had no idea."

Ragnar gave a humorless chuckle. "Those were hard days. Thankfully, Theta started to make enough so I could quit my second job and focus on it full time. And shortly thereafter, we found out we were having a baby. We agreed that Zuri would stay home with Sophie, but I can't tell you how stressed I was back then."

Magnus said, "Now I really feel like a whiner. I'm grateful for all that God's given us. The business is growing, and I hope this—" he gestured at the documents and legal pads scattered across the table, "will help us grow even more."

Ragnar nodded. "I really hope so. I mean, I've had some success, but I haven't made a killing like you have. I'm worth peanuts compared to you."

Magnus laughed and Ragnar said, "No, seriously. These are facts. God has brought me a long way, but I still need to hustle. I have Sophie, to provide for, of course, and if things go the way I hope, Ella and Tiffany will be part of my life as well." He smiled. "Maybe we'll have some more children."

He paused for a moment. "She's never come out and said it and I don't think she wants to talk about it, but I get the sense that her husband left her struggling. She has that house in Reigate, but it's got a massive mortgage and she's been doing transcription and other piecework like that to make ends meet. And living on the generosity of her mother-in-law as well," he added.

Ragnar gathered up his notebooks and paperwork. "I want to take care of them. I don't want her to ever worry again about finances, about college tuition costs for her daughter, about keeping a roof over her head. So, yeah, I'm praying this big idea of yours will be a success."

"Amen to that," Magnus said. "Sounds like things are going well with you and Ella."

Ragnar smiled. "I think so. I mean, it's not like the first go around when you just jump in with no idea what you're in for and you have very little baggage behind you. We're blending a family and we have to be really intentional and careful with every step."

"What do you mean by intentional?" Magnus asked.

"Well, for one thing, we started having sessions with our pastor as soon as we decided to begin dating. He says it's really important for us to recognize that we both come with the trauma of losing our spouses, and we also have patterns of behavior from our previous marriages. He said in some ways we would have to put aside the positive memories and patterns too, because this is a whole new person and we can't expect them to be just like our previous spouse was."

Magnus's eyes widened. "Wow, that is complicated."

"Yeah," Ragnar said. "But in a way it's good to know right up front that we have to work at it."

"I can see that," Magnus said. He put the last of his documents into his briefcase. "Right, I'm off."

"I'll work from home tomorrow," Ragnar said. "Try to get a start on this research. Maybe we can touch base tomorrow and figure out when to meet again."

"Sounds good," Magnus said. "And I think Nia was planning to call you to set up a date when you can bring Ella and Tiffany over to our place."

"Great, I look forward to hearing from her," Ragnar said. They walked out of the room.

Ragnar headed down to the underground car park, glad that he'd had the foresight to drive himself into London today instead of taking the train. If he had come by public transport, he would probably have been stuck in town today, since he was pretty sure that the last train for Hatbrook had already left just after midnight.

He opened the passenger door and set down his briefcase before going around to the driver's seat. He was exhilarated by how well the plans were coming together with

Magnus and Nordic Wind. It had been ages since he'd felt this excited about anything business-related. He could feel the creative juices and ideas flowing through him, just like in the early days when he was founding Theta Software. The thrill of beginning something new, of conquering a new endeavor, energized him like nothing else.

He couldn't wait to share his feelings with Ella about the latest progress they had made. A warm rush of emotions flooded through him as he thought about her. Earlier when he had called to tell her that he was going to be late once again and would need her to have Sophie sleep over at her place, she had accepted it quietly and without fuss.

She was such a blessing for him and for Sophie. His daughter adored her, and he felt peaceful and grateful knowing that Sophie was under her watchful care while he worked late. He was determined to do his best to build a strong financial foundation for his family's security, a family that he hoped would include Ella and Tiffany. God willing, all of this hard work and late hours was going to pay off.

Chapter Twenty-Five

ELLA STOOD WITH her phone in her hand, unable to believe what Ragnar was saying. She slid the door open and walked out into her back yard, so the girls, who were building a puzzle on the living room floor, would not hear her side of the conversation.

She fought for control of her voice as she spoke to him. "But the girls are looking forward to going to the cinema with you. They've been excited about this for days."

Ragnar's voice was apologetic. "I know, and I'm sorry. But one of our potential backers just had an unexpected opening in his schedule and is coming in to see us to talk about the new biologics department. Having him on board would be an incredible boost for us, and it could be weeks until he has free time again. This really has to be done today while we have the chance."

Ella closed her eyes. "So I have to tell them you're not coming?"

"Is it possible to put it off until tomorrow?" he asked.

"I've already got the tickets."

Ragnar said, "I'm sorry. I'll make it up to them. I'll take them to the trampoline park at the weekend instead."

Ella gripped the phone and was silent for a moment, wondering how to say what was on her mind without sounding whiny. Ragnar said, "Ella? Are you there?"

"Yes, I'm here."

"I wouldn't have canceled if it wasn't important. But this is a huge opportunity we can't pass up. He's cleared his evening for us."

"His evening? Does this mean you're going to be late back again?" Ella asked.

Ragnar said, "Hopefully not. I should be back around seven."

Ella suppressed a sigh. "Okay. Sophie can have dinner with us. I hope the meeting goes well."

"Thank you. And sorry once again," he said. "I'll make sure to do something with the girls at the weekend."

Ella took the girls to the cinema. They were thrilled by the movie, but she couldn't follow the storyline. The bouncy, cheerful music,

cartoonish capers and wild hijinks passed over her head.

A growing and familiar sense of dread gnawed at her gut, lurking in the back of her mind like a dark storm cloud whose contours she recognized all too well. She tried to reason her unease away. It was just a movie. Cinemas showed them every day. And Ragnar's explanation had been perfectly reasonable. He needed to do something important. But his bailing out of plans seemed to be happening more and more often. It was always for a really good reason: an emergency with his old company, a meeting that ran long, or, like today, a last-minute opportunity that he needed to grab before it was gone.

But she had the feeling of being pushed further and further down the priority list. That had been a common occurrence with Neil. She and Tiffany had been like placeholders, penciled into Neil's agenda until something better, more interesting, or more rewarding came along for him. Then they were just shunted out of the way while he went after the new thing.

Macey's words came back, her allegations about Ragnar's single-minded focus on his work, and how he had treated his wife. Ella wanted to shake off the thoughts, to push them away. But it was getting harder with every canceled appointment, every new request to have Sophie sleep over while he worked late.

It was approaching nine o'clock that evening when Ella opened the door in answer to Ragnar's knock. His tie was pulled loose, and he held his suit jacket draped over his arm. He bent over and touched her lips with his, his arms encircling her.

"I've just been able to get away. Thanks for having Sophie again. They already asleep?"

"Probably," Ella said. "They were pretty tired, so I put them down."

"Can I just look in on her?" Ragnar asked. He walked down the hallway and pushed the door open, poking his head into the room. He stepped inside and Ella went into the living room and sank onto her sofa.

Ragnar came back out. "She's fast asleep," he said.

Ella clasped her hands in her lap. She looked up at him. "Ragnar, this is the second night in a row she's gone to bed without seeing you." Her voice was gentle, and she tried to keep any accusing note out.

He sat down heavily in an armchair and ran his hands through his hair. "I know. I don't like it, either." He rubbed his temples. "I'll do my best to be here earlier tomorrow, and I'll take them out at the weekend. Did you go to the movie?"

"Yes. They loved it," Ella said. "But, Ragnar..." she struggled to find the words to say. "I feel like we hardly have family time these days."

Ragnar crossed over to sit next to her. "I really am sorry about today. It was a one-off thing." He looked into her eyes. "Will you forgive me?"

She nodded and let him wrap her in his arms. It was much easier than trying to explain her growing unease. He held her for a long moment, then said, "Tell me about your day. Any news about the house?"

"I heard from Charles. He's put in much more stringent vetting requirement for new tenants, and it's taking a lot longer than I'd hoped to find anyone suitable."

"I don't blame him for being extra careful," Ragnar said. "But it's costing you money having the house stand vacant."

"I know," Ella said. Between her transcription pay and childminding fees she was keeping her basic costs covered. Her rent guarantee insurance was paying for most of the mortgage, but she needed to get tenants in place before the insurance term ended.

"Are you sure you want to keep renting it out?" Ragnar asked. "You could just sell it."

Ella remembered Jocelyn's reaction when she'd mentioned selling Neil's house. "I'd like to keep it for now."

"Fair enough," Ragnar said. "I'm sure your agent's doing his best. What did you and the girls get up to today?"

He gave her his full attention while she talked about how she and the girls had spent their day, and she felt herself relaxing. Ragnar had the ability to be fully present when he was with her, and to make her feel like every word she was saying mattered to him.

Even as she talked, the thought ran in the back of her mind that Neil had never made her feel like that. It will be okay, she told herself, as she leaned into the arm that he held around her shoulders.

Chapter Twenty-Six

A COUPLE OF weeks later on a Friday afternoon, Ella smiled as she let Vanya into Ragnar's living room. "Hi! Come in," she said.

Vanya walked inside and gave her a quick hug. "The first thing I want to do is take these off!" She kicked off her high-heeled pumps and rubbed one foot. "That feels so good!"

"Thanks so much for coming over," Ella said, leading the way into the living room. She and Ragnar had an appointment with Pastor Jonathan, after which they had plans for dinner and a movie. Vanya was going to watch the girls while they were out.

"Is Ragnar not here yet?" Vanya asked.

"No," Ella said. "He said he'd be back by five, though."

Ella liked Vanya. When she'd first met Ragnar's sister, she had been intimidated by her poise, immaculate grooming, and expensive clothes. While she'd never given much thought to the differences between her and Ragnar's upbringing, Vanya was a stark reminder of the privileged background he'd come from. But she'd soon learned that what she'd thought of as reserve in Vanya was in fact shyness, and that behind her polished and cold veneer, Vanya had a warm heart and was eager to know her older brother's girlfriend. Tiffany had liked her immediately.

"Go ahead and do what you need to, and I'll hang out with the girls," Vanya said. "Where are they?"

"On the trampoline," Ella said. "And I'm pretty much ready. I've prepared a tuna casserole for the girls' dinner. It's on the counter, and you'll just need to pop it into the oven for about half an hour."

"Is it fool-proof?" Vanya asked. "You know I can't cook!"

Ella laughed. "Yes, it's fool-proof. Thirty minutes at one hundred eighty degrees. Check it at twenty minutes, though, and you can take it out if it looks golden brown on the top. I'm not used to Ragnar's oven. I'll write that on a note, if you'd like."

"Please do," Vanya said.

Ella went to the kitchen and found a notepad. She scribbled the instructions, then glanced up at the clock. It was ten minutes to five. Ragnar was cutting it close.

Half an hour later, Ella paced up and down the living room and tried to restrain herself from checking her watch again. Where was he?

She tried to avoid Vanya's eyes. Ragnar's sister sat at the kitchen table with the girls, helping Sophie and Tiffany sprinkle glitter onto their craft project. "What color do you want next?" Vanya asked. "Gold? All right, sweetheart." Vanya popped open the gold glitter tube and handed it to Tiffany.

She looked up at Ella, sympathy in her blue eyes. "Maybe he's stuck in traffic. There was a lot of roadwork when I was driving up here, and I had to use a detour."

Yes, but you still managed to get here on time, Ella thought. She checked her watch and looked out the window again. "That might be it. It would help if his phone was turned on so we could find out what was going on. I really can't wait any longer. I expect he's just around the corner, but I think I'd better go on ahead to Pastor Jonathan's office. If he comes here, would you let him know that I already left?"

"Of course," Vanya said. "I'll send him off with a flea in his ear."

Ella managed a weak smile and grabbed her purse. She got into her car and made the short drive to the church office with five minutes to spare. She scanned the entrance to the parking lot, expecting to see Ragnar pulling in. She got out her phone. Still no message from Ragnar, and no missed call. She tried his number again, but it was still switched off. She guessed that his battery had probably gone flat. Should she wait out here or go in?

This was supposed to be their third session with Pastor Jonathan. In their previous chats with him, they spent time talking about their pasts and their expectations for their new relationship. She found it helpful to articulate some of her thoughts, although she still felt a barrier about revealing too much about her life with Neil. But Pastor Jonathan's gentle probing had opened avenues of discussion which seemed to be helping her and Ragnar move forward in their relationship.

She checked the time again and saw that she couldn't wait any longer. She let herself into the building and walked down to the church office. Beryl, the pastor's secretary, was just packing up her things, since she usually left by five o'clock. "Hi, Ella," she said with a big smile. "Good to see you. You're looking very well, indeed. Pastor Jonathan is waiting."

"Thank you," Ella said.

She went into the office. Pastor Jonathan stood by the window, nose buried in a hardcover book. He looked up and smiled at Ella, his wispy hair looking even more chaotic today, framing his long face like a halo. "Wonderful to see you today, Ella." He looked past her into the open and empty doorway. "Is Ragnar not here?"

Ella shook her head. "No. He seems to be running late and his phone isn't on. I left a message that he should come straight here."

"All right, that does happen sometimes," Pastor Jonathan said. "The commute from London can be brutal." He walked to the door and leaned out. "Beryl, I know that you were preparing to go. Would you mind just waiting a few minutes until Ragnar comes in? We're expecting him any moment."

Beryl's voice floated in through the open doorway. "No problem, Pastor Jonathan, as long as it's not too long. Will ten minutes do? I really can't stay any longer than that."

"I expect ten minutes should be okay," Pastor Jonathan said.

He pulled the door back, leaving it halfway open. Ella knew that it wasn't personal; he always operated by the Billy Graham rule. It meant that he was always extremely careful whenever he met with anyone for counseling. As a matter of principle, he didn't want to be alone with her unless either Beryl or Ragnar was present.

He crossed back to his desk and sat down. "Shall we give him a few more minutes?"

Ella nodded, hands twisting in her lap. Every minute seemed to last an eternity, and he passed the time by asking her general questions about how she had been, and how the homeschooling was going with Tiffany. Finally, when ten minutes had passed, Pastor Jonathan looked at the doorway again and rubbed his chin. "Well, I wonder," he said softly. He bowed his head for a moment then looked up at Ella. "Could you try to reach out to him again?"

Ella pulled out her phone and re-dialed Ragnar's number. The call went straight to voicemail. She looked up at Pastor Jonathan and shook her head, unable to trust her voice.

Pastor Jonathan bowed his head again, then stood up. "I'm really sorry. We'll have to try to arrange this again for another time. Beryl has to leave now; I can't keep her any longer."

Ella nodded. She struggled to her feet, clutching her purse and her phone. "Sorry. Thanks," she whispered.

She walked out of the office, nodding at Beryl as she passed her desk, praying for enough strength to hold her tears back until she was safely in her car. She made it to the driver's seat and leaned on the steering wheel, face buried in her hands. She couldn't hold back any longer. Sobs shook her shoulders.

Chapter Twenty-Seven

TWO HOURS LATER, Ella sat at her kitchen counter. Vanya and the girls were still at Ragnar's house. She had left them watching a movie and gone back to her empty apartment, desperate for space and quiet to think.

Alone, without having to worry about the children seeing her, she let her mind range unchecked over what had happened tonight.

Macey's warning kept coming back to her. "Ragnar has always been like this, had this tendency to get obsessed with his work... Zuri told me she felt like she and even their child came at the bottom of his priority list... There was always some urgent business issue or other to deal with."

The shadow of dread that had never been completely banished took shape again. She couldn't hide from the truth anymore. Ragnar was showing her what he was like. He was stirring up dark feelings she'd kept bottled up since her marriage to Neil. Neil's plans and wishes had always come first, and she was just an accessory to his life, to be picked up when needed, but otherwise discarded and forgotten. Just like a child's toy that doesn't have a life of its own until it's time to be played with.

She hadn't seen it at first because in the beginning, she had been Neil's shiny new object, his fad of the moment. She'd mistaken his transient infatuation for devotion.

She'd been too blinkered by her own all-consuming adoration for him to see what was happening. And now the same thing was happening with Ragnar. He was already relegating her to nothing more than a support role for his priorities. He was seeing less and less of his own daughter as well because he was so focused on his own new obsession.

There was a knock at her door. Ragnar stood there, face flushed, hands held up.

"Ella, I'm so sorry. I completely forgot about this afternoon. My phone battery had gone flat, and when I got home, Vanya reminded me."

She stepped back inside, and he followed her down the hall and into the living room, still spilling out his apology. "I can't believe I forgot our meeting. I don't know where my head was."

She turned to face him, shoulders squared. "Ragnar, I can't do this anymore."

He looked at her, his gray eyes wide. "Can't do what?"

"I can't let myself keep leaning on someone who is always letting me down."

"What?" The color drained from his face, then rushed back in a flood.

"I'm constantly holding my breath, waiting to get bumped off your list. Something is always coming up. A meeting, a client, an emergency. Oh, I know it's always important. And I completely understand that. But it's just killing me inside."

He crossed the room with quick steps, holding out his arms. She raised her hands to ward him off. She didn't want him to touch her. He would hold her, and she would crumble and start to cry and wouldn't be able to get her words out.

"No, please don't," she said.

"Ella, please," he said. "I'm sorry, I made a huge mistake today. I—"

"It's not just today," she said. "It's been happening over and over. When was the last time you put Sophie to bed?"

A spasm of pain crossed his face. "I... Thursday?"

"It was Tuesday," she said. "Three days ago. And each time you had a perfectly good reason. But it just builds up and builds up."

He looked as though he'd just had a kick in the guts. He sat down, rubbing his temples with his fingers. "Okay, I get it. Things have been crazy lately. But it will settle down." He looked up at her. "I'm so close to setting something up that will be wonderful for our future. That's why I'm doing this."

He stood up again and stepped closer to her. "Ella, I've been waiting for the right time to tell you this. I love you. I want you to be my wife. I want to spend the rest of my life with you, taking care of you and Tiffany. That's why I've been working so hard. I want us to have financial stability, so we never have to worry about the children's education or us growing old. I know that's not an excuse, especially for today. But I love you, Ella. With every fiber inside me."

"Don't say that!" she shouted, pressing her hands against her ears. Her eyes were hot with tears. "Don't use love against me. Neil said he loved me. Maybe he even believed that he did. But he never put us first. What he wanted, what he felt was important, took priority. Every single time. Words mean nothing when what you actually do says something completely different."

She looked at his ashen face and drew in a shaky breath. "You don't love me, Ragnar. You love what I can do for you. You love how I can take care of your daughter and your home and make it possible for you to go out and do what you really love."

"That's not true," he said, his voice raw. "You're the reason I'm working so hard. It's because I'm trying to take care of you. I know I really messed things up. I got so caught up in what I was trying to do that I failed to see that. But I can change things. I'll try to limit the hours I work. I'll be home in time for dinner."

"Did you change for Zuri?"

"What?"

"Did you limit your working hours, get home in time for dinner, be there for your wife and your daughter when you were married to Zuri?"

He froze. "What do you know about Zuri?"

"Macey told me what things were like," Ella said. Remembering her friend's words strengthened her resolve, and she spoke with an edge in her voice. "She said Zuri felt alone. She said you were hardly there. You were busy working, building up your business. That sounds very familiar. She said you missed almost every prenatal appointment when Zuri was pregnant with Sophie. And you know something funny? I know exactly what that feels like. Neil missed pretty much all of mine as well. At least you were working hard. Your excuses are a lot better; I'll give you that much. You weren't out partying with your friends. But the end result is there's a wife at home who needs her husband and is alone."

He turned away from her and walked toward the window. His shoulders sagged as he passed a hand over his eyes. He turned around, his mouth moving as though to form words. She could see the agony on his face. It matched the knife-like pain in her heart.

"I believe everything you say you want to do, Ragnar." Her voice cracked, but she pushed on. "I even believe that you think you love me. And I love you. But you'll make me lean on you and count on you. And then when I need you the most, when I need you to be there for me, you'll be taking care of something else. I just can't do that. I can't set myself up for that again. Leaning on Neil broke me. And I won't let you do that to me." She felt a tear escape and run down her cheek. She brushed it away impatiently. She didn't want to cry. If she started, she wouldn't stop.

"Maybe I'm too needy," she said. "Maybe I should just woman up and be okay with you never being around. But I know that I can't. I need my husband to put his family first in a way that I can see. And you need somebody who'll be fine with you being away so much. Maybe we're just not right for each other."

His cheeks were wet with tears. He held his hands out again, palms upwards, as though in prayer. "Can't we work it out? We can talk to someone, see a counselor. Let's speak to Pastor Jonathan. We could make it work."

"We have been talking to Pastor Jonathan. And here we are," she said. "I'm sorry, but I have to protect myself and Tiffany. It's over, Ragnar. I'm stopping it before it goes too far and hurts us even more."

She turned her back on him. She couldn't stand to look at his face anymore. The expression in his eyes looked too much like anguish. "Please send Tiffany over when you get back home."

She heard his footsteps head toward the door and the click of the lock as he went out.

Chapter Twenty-Eight

RAGNAR CLOSED HIS front door behind him and stood in the hallway, his ears ringing, his stomach in knots. He stared in front of him.

Vanya called out, "Is that you, Ragnar?" When he didn't respond, she came toward the door from the living room. "Oh, it was you. I—" she stopped short when she saw his face. Her expression changed. "Are you okay?"

He didn't answer and went to the bottom of the staircase. "Are the girls upstairs?"

"Yes. Is Ella coming back? It's getting close to bedtime for the girls."

Ragnar roused himself, shaking his head as though to clear it. "No, she's not coming." He called up the stairs. "Tiffany, it's home time now."

Tiffany came down the staircase, Sophie behind her. The knife in his heart twisted as he looked at Tiffany.

"Already?" she asked.

"Yes. Grab your shoes and I'll walk you home," he said. He didn't know how his voice was able to come across so calm when inside, he was screaming with agony.

"Okay. Bye, Sophie. Bye, Vanya." Tiffany went to the front hallway and pushed her feet into her purple Crocs.

Vanya was watching him. She stepped forward and said, "I'll walk you home, Tiffany."

He breathed a silent thanks to her, then said to his daughter, "Sophie, would you brush your teeth and get ready for bed? I'll be up in a minute to tuck you in."

"Can I have a story, Dad?"

"Yes, of course." He watched her go up the stairs.

Words from his talk with Ella flew through his head like a movie reel scrolling at light speed, but he fixated on one sentence. "Macey told me what things were like." Macey. What had she said to Ella? What did she have to do with all this?

Vanya came back into the house, and he turned to face her. "I need to go out after I've settled Sophie. Would you mind staying here for a little bit? I'll try not to be more than an hour."

"Okay," she said. "But is everything all right?"

"No. Ella just finished things with me."

"What?" Vanya's eyes were wide. "Just now?"

"Yes. I'd rather not talk about it," he said, keeping his voice low.

"Dad, I'm ready for my story," Sophie called from upstairs.

"Coming," Ragnar said. He went upstairs and read her latest favorite book, *What The Ladybird Heard*. The words barely registered and his voice sounded mechanical in his own ears, but Sophie seemed happy with it and linked her small arms around his neck.

"Can I have another one, Dad?"

"Not tonight, sweetheart. It's late. Let's have our prayer time." Sophie folded her hands and squeezed her eyes shut.

Ragnar prayed out loud, "Lord, thank you for today, and thank you for taking care of us. Help us to have a good sleep with no nightmares and help us to wake up fresh for a new day tomorrow. Amen."

He was about to stand up when Sophie continued the prayer, "And, Lord Jesus, please bless my best friend Tiffany and Ella and Auntie Vanya and everyone. Amen."

Ragnar's heart constricted. How was he going to tell her about Ella and Tiffany? He'd probably need to find some other childcare. Sophie was going to be an innocent casualty of his breakup. He bent over and kissed her forehead, keeping his eyes averted so she wouldn't see the moisture in them. "Good night, sweetheart," he said, then turned the light off.

He went back downstairs, walking past Vanya as he picked up his car keys. "I'll be back soon. Thanks for staying."

He ignored the unspoken question he could see her face and headed out to his car. The only person he wanted to talk to right now was Macey. He needed to know what she had been filling Ella's head with, what stories she'd been spreading about Zuri. He knew exactly where Macey lived, in a small apartment block about ten minutes away. She hadn't moved since she and Zuri had been friends.

He found a spot in the parking lot and pulled in. He remembered that she lived on the third floor. He took the stairs, two at a time, and walked up to the second door on the right side of the hallway. He rang the doorbell, then rapped on the door.

Macey pulled the door open, and her eyebrows flew up. "Ragnar! What are you doing here?"

"Have you got a minute?"

She crossed her arms. "Yes. Just one. What is it about?"

"Can I come in?"

She made room for him to walk past her. Her apartment hadn't changed much since he had last been here. His gaze snagged on a framed picture that hung on a wall. It was Macey and Zuri in a candid shot, laughing uproariously.

He turned and faced her. He forced himself to keep his breath and his voice steady. "I won't take much of your time. What did you say to Ella about Zuri?"

Macey's eyes narrowed. "What did I tell Ella? I told her the truth. About how we were friends and what Zuri said to me about you."

"And what exactly was that?" Ragnar asked. He could feel a muscle twitch in his cheek.

She stood her ground, arms akimbo. "About what a workaholic you were. About all the time she spent on her own because building your business seemed to mean more to you than building your marriage."

Heat rushed up to his face and a wave of anger blazed up inside him. "You had absolutely no right."

"I had every right," she shot back. "Zuri was my best friend. I watched month after month as you just neglected the best wife in the world and your amazing child because you were so caught up trying to chase the big bucks. Well, you got the big bucks. I hope it was worth it."

Ragnar clenched his fists. "That's not true. Zuri knew why I had to work so hard. She knew that I was starting off with nothing. I was going flat out because we needed to eat and keep the electricity on. She knew what it would take to get my business started."

"Yes, she did know that you'd have to work hard, and she was grateful for everything you did. But here's the thing: lots of people have to work hard. But most people, no matter how busy they may be, don't miss the birth of their first child because they were at a business meeting."

"I didn't miss Sophie's birth," he said.

"No, you were there for the last ten minutes. I was the one she called when her water broke. She'd tried to reach you first but couldn't get a hold of you. I took her to the hospital. I was with her for fourteen hours. Your phone was turned off because you were with some client and your secretary couldn't reach you. Who turns their phone off when their wife is forty weeks pregnant?"

Ragnar ran his hand through his hair. He could justify what he did, but every excuse he had would sound hollow. The client he'd met with that day ended up giving Theta Software their first major contract, one that finally put the company on the map and brought a string of referrals. But how could he lay that up against the birth of his child?

Macey wasn't waiting for an answer, anyway. She plowed on, relentless as a juggernaut. "And then after that you took, what, one morning off to bring her home from the hospital? She was in that house on her own with a brand-new baby and you were right back working twelve-hour days. I loved Zuri. And I love Ella. I know a bit of what she went through with Neil. From what she's told me, he was the most selfish piece of work imaginable. Charming, but completely self-absorbed. Want to buy a new designer jacket this month? Oh, we'll just grab that and let Ella deal with it when the electricity gets cut off. How about a fancy boys-only holiday with your pals at a luxury Maui resort? Pop it onto a new credit card next to the five others we've already maxed out. And don't forget to go skydiving when you know that your life and holiday insurance don't cover dangerous sports. Who cares what will happen to your wife and child when things go wrong? Yolo, right? You only live once. She'll pick up the pieces again when the insurance doesn't pay out."

Ragnar stared at Macey, his mouth dry. "Ella's husband did that?"

"She didn't tell you?" Macey said.

"No," Ragnar said. "She's never said much to me about him. But I'm nothing like that. Doesn't she realize that? There's a huge difference between not being there because you're partying and working long hours because you're providing for your family."

"Oh no, of course." Macey's tone had a biting edge. "You've got the best excuse in the world for neglecting your wife. You are doing it all for her. How could she complain when you're working so hard to keep a roof over her head and put food on her table? She should just keep quiet and take it and be grate- ful. Why wouldn't anyone want to be married to an ATM?"

The bitterness in her voice stung him. Is that what Zuri had thought? Had Zuri told her this about him?

"And you said all this to Ella?"

"I did. But I was a bit more dip- lomatic with her. I'm not bothering to sugarcoat it for you. I've seen how you operate, going after these soft-hearted, submissive women who have no family support and no one else to lean on but you. Oh, and I told her all this before you guys started dating. So, she decided to be with you even though she knew."

Ragnar stared at her, fists clenched, anger flooding his body like liquid fire. Her face was hard, her dark eyes like obsidian. He snarled, "Well, you'll probably be glad to know that she's dumped me. So, job well done."

Her eyes widened, and her jaw hung open. Ragnar stalked to the door and let himself out.

Chapter Twenty-Nine

ELLA WENT THROUGH Tiffany's bedtime routine on autopilot. When her daughter was finally settled, she made herself a cup of tea, then sat at the kitchen counter, staring at nothing while the tea grew cold. She kept seeing Ragnar's face. His eyes, like deep gray pools of pain. She had done that to him. Lacerated him with her words. But she needed to amputate their relationship quickly, in one heavy stroke.

"You did the right thing," Ella whispered. She tried to believe her own words. But if she'd done the right thing, why did she feel as though she had just taken a flamethrower and torched something precious? Her heart ached so much that she wondered how she was going to bear it. Tears spilled onto her cheeks.

She forced herself to remember what it had been like with Neil. She had cut Ragnar off because she didn't want to repeat the same heartache.

Things had started off wonderfully with Neil as well. In the early days of their relationship, swept on an intoxicating wave, she felt as though their love could conquer anything. They had gotten married while riding the crest of that wave, and the early months of their marriage were pure bliss. Then, almost imperceptibly at first, she began to notice things that she hadn't seen before. Or, perhaps she had seen them but had pushed him to the back of her mind.

Neil's impulsiveness, coming in the form of spur of the moment trips and extravagant gifts, had been exciting at first. But she soon began to see how it fell into a pattern of instant gratification, where he did what he wanted and got what he wanted the moment he wanted it.

Neil grew bored after the first heady feelings of the honeymoon period settled into the routine of building a marriage, and he'd started seeking new thrills elsewhere. The thrills took a darker turn when he began hanging out with the group of friends with whom he'd eventually gone to Maui. She knew they'd experimented with drugs, and she suspected there had been at least one affair.

Just like Ragnar, Neil had at first insisted that he loved her. Then he'd started missing the occasional family dinner, staying out later, being away the odd weekend. No big deal at first. But his absences increased until him being away was the new normal. Ragnar was following the same pattern. More and more of his time being taken up by work projects until his being home in time for dinner, his free weekends, began to dwindle into the exception rather than the rule. He had begun canceling or forgetting important appointments, and they weren't even married yet.

She knew that Ragnar was not the same kind of pleasure-seeking impulsive man that Neil had been. Work seemed to be his drug of choice. Neither he nor Neil had the concept of balance. That was why she had to stop it now, before she was in too deep. But the agony she felt made her wonder whether she was already in too deep, whether cutting him off was going to be a blow that she could survive.

And what about Sophie? The thought of his daughter brought tears rushing to Ella's eyes. She had grown to love that little girl. Who wouldn't? She was adorable and so sweet and trusting. Caring for her was an absolute pleasure, and she had thought it would be wonderful to be her stepmother. But what was going to happen to Sophie now?

She touched her cup, noticing how cold the tea had become. She looked up at the clock. It was almost four in the morning. Had she been sitting here that long? She dumped the tea into the sink.

She couldn't carry on being Sophie's child-minder. And living across the road from Ragnar had been wonderful when they were just friends and even better when they were a couple. But it would be unbearable now that they'd split up, especially since their daughters had become so used to spending just about all day and every day together. How was she going to handle that?

Ella forced herself through the motions of getting ready for bed. She needed to try to get at least some sleep. It was Saturday tomorrow. Not an official child-minding day, so she could put Tiffany into the car and drive off somewhere. Let Ragnar tell Sophie whatever he felt was most appropriate.

Ragnar pulled into his driveway and went inside. The house was quiet, and the living room and kitchen were empty. He went upstairs and saw a bar of light under the guest room door. Vanya had clearly decided to spend the night.

He went into his bedroom and sat on his bed, covering his face with his hands. "Oh, God—" he started, but an aching lump blocked his throat. Pain ripped inside him, exploding out into sobs he couldn't control. He buried his face in a pillow to muffle the sounds, and his bed shook as he released his anguish in a torrent of tears.

Zuri was gone forever, after hiding from him heartache that he had caused.

And now Ella was gone. Ella, whose gentle sweetness had brought a new hope into his life, believed that he didn't love her. The words she had flung at him burned like acid in his heart. "You don't love me, Ragnar. You love what I can do for you. You love how I can take care of your daughter and your home and make it possible for you to go out and do what you really love."

How could she think that? How had he managed to hurt her so badly that even though she said she loved him, she would rather be alone than be with him? His mind groped in the dark, struggling to understand, grasping for the link between his and her past and why things had fallen to pieces now.

And Macey. She'd held up a mirror to him that showed a grotesque reflection of himself and how he treated the women he loved. If Macey was speaking the truth, he'd caused Zuri pain as well, neglecting her during his push to get his business off the ground. He was following the same pattern now, letting his business appointments and long working hours crowd his life, leaving less and less space for Sophie and Ella.

But there was more to it than that. Ella had mentioned Neil, and so had Macey. Ragnar held only fragments of information about Ella's former husband, but from what he was piecing together, the marriage hadn't been a happy one. He thought of Ella, bruised and scarred by the man who claimed he loved her. So wounded that she thought that Ragnar was going to do the same thing.

A memory came to him from his childhood, of when he'd found an injured bird in his grandmother's back yard. He couldn't remember what kind of bird it had been, but its wing was broken and it sat shivering on the ground. He'd wanted to pick it up, but his grandmother told him that unless he was very gentle, stress and fear could do as much harm to the bird as whatever injury it originally had. In its terror and pain, the bird didn't know how much he longed to get it out of harm's way and help it.

With a flash of insight, he realized that Ella was like that bird. She was broken and hurting and couldn't see inside his heart. He'd failed to show her how deeply he loved her. He had been so sure that God had brought her into his life. She fit in so beautifully. She seemed perfect, not just for him, but for Sophie as well. Had he been badly mistaken?

He began to pray, laying out his anguish before God. At first, he cried out to God about his own heartache, but his words turned into a stream of intercession for Ella, a river of prayer mixed with his own tears. "Lord, I don't know what's in her past, what brokenness and pain she's carrying. Forgive me for adding to it. I pray that you would heal her, bring her to complete wholeness. Even if her future doesn't involve me, I ask you to put her back together inside. Give her real happiness and joy. Let her truly know your tender love for her."

When he finished praying, he stretched out on his bed utterly spent, drained, and wrung out, but at peace. He remembered the verse that he had lived on, the one that had carried him through the waking nightmare of Zuri's death. Psalm 34:18. ***"The Lord is nigh unto them that are of a broken heart."*** God had been close to him then, and He would continue to be close to him now. There was pain now, but it would be okay.

Chapter Thirty

ELLA WOKE UP to the sound of a loud knocking on her door, and the ringing of her doorbell. She struggled out of bed and pulled on her robe.

Tiffany was standing in the hallway in her pajamas. "There's someone at the door, Mum, but you told me I should never open it to anyone."

"That's right, sweetheart," Ella said, stroking her daughter's cheek as she walked past her. She opened the front door. Jocelyn stood there, looking tanned and trim, her hair freshly cut and highlighted.

"Hi, dear. Did I wake you?" Jocelyn reached out and hugged her. "Jarvis and I just landed back from Greece and I wanted to say a quick hello. Hi, Tiffany, darling!"

Tiffany came running to the door at the sound of her grandmother's voice. "Hi, Nana!"

Jocelyn scooped her up and gave her a squeeze. "Look at you! It's been ages since your Nana saw you. You've grown so much!"

Ella said, "How was your stay? Do you want to come in?"

"Oh, no, don't worry. I just wanted to say hi. We had a marvelous time. And, um..." She paused and waggled her left hand in front of Ella's face. A white gold ring with a double row of diamonds sparkled on her third finger. To Ella's open-mouthed expression, Jocelyn squealed, "Jarvis and I got married!"

Ella was stunned. She cast about for words to say but couldn't think of any that would not sound insincere. How could Jocelyn have married that walking bag of sleaze? "Congratulations," she finally stammered. "That's a real surprise."

"I know!" Jocelyn said. "We'd been talking about it for a bit. Then when we were over in Greece, we decided, why not just go for it? So, we eloped to Corfu and had the ceremony there. Jarvis will be moving in with me since my place is bigger and the trains to London go a lot more often from Hatbrook."

Ella could hardly think of any news she would have welcomed less. It was bad enough when Jarvis had been Jocelyn's partner and she only had to see him occasionally, but now he was going to be a permanent fixture next door. "Uh huh," she said. Her mouth refused to obey the command to smile.

"Stop by later and I'll show you the photos," Jocelyn said. She turned to Tiffany. "And I've got a stack of presents for you, sweetheart! But you'll have to come to Nana's place and see them."

"Yay!" Tiffany said, clapping her hands.

"Is Jarvis there now?" Ella asked.

"No, he's gone to his apartment to take care of some things. He'll come by this evening." Jocelyn looked at Ella with narrowed eyes. "And it looks like I caught you in bed, then. Were you having a lie-in? Haven't got any, um, company, have you?"

Ella caught her meaning, and heat rushed to her face. "No, of course not."

"No. You're both good Christians, aren't you? Well, I'll see you later. I just wanted to tell you our news, and let you know that we're back. Maybe we can make plans for you and your young man to come over for a meal. I'd like to get to know him better. But I'd better go now.

See you soon." Jocelyn fluttered her fingers and turned to walk back to her house.

Ella closed the door. All the air and light were being sucked out of her life. Instead of having Ragnar as her new dad, Tiffany was getting Jarvis as a grandfather. A wave of sadness hit her, so powerful that she had to lean against the door to keep her footing. She closed her eyes to stop the tears from slipping out.

"Are you okay, Mum?" Tiffany asked.

"I'm fine, sweetheart," Ella said, fighting to keep her voice steady. "Get your clothes on and I'll pour you a bowl of cereal."

As Tiffany went to her room, Ella took several slow breaths. She had managed to live before Ragnar, and she was going to survive with him out of her life, even though every heartbeat without him hurt like an eternity of torment. Her fists clenched, she straightened her back, squared her shoulders, and went into the kitchen.

Ragnar jolted awake. For a moment, he couldn't think where he was. He was lying on top of his bed, still fully clothed, his Bible in his hand. He had crashed last night, too exhausted to get into bed. He swung his legs over the side of his bed and sat up. His mind rushed straight to Ella and his crushing sorrow over losing her.

Images and voices flooded his head as he stood and paced the floor. She said it was over, and he wanted to respect her choice. Last night, he had meant it with all his heart when he prayed that God would give her a good life even though it didn't include him. If the door truly was closed on his relationship with her, he would find a way to let her go, even though it killed him. He had released her into God's hands, and he would walk away if he had to.

But he didn't want to. He couldn't let go yet. A woman like her was more precious than rubies. He wasn't willing to give her up. He had had a virtuous wife before and having another such woman cross his path was more than he had ever dreamed possible. He couldn't let her slip through his hands. Not without a fight. A knock-down, drag out fight where he left everything out on the battlefield.

He stopped his pacing and stood still. What would it take to get her back? What would it cost him? Was he willing to pay the price? Love wasn't cheap. The Bible commanded men to love their wives as Christ loved the church. Christ had loved with a sacrificial love that was willing to abase itself and give up everything. If he claimed to love Ella, to aspire to the priceless privilege of being her husband, it was going to cost him everything he had. And he would pay it willingly.

Chapter Thirty-One

ELLA STARED AT the phone in her hand for close to a minute before she took a deep breath and dialed Charles Appleton.

"Hello Mrs. Belmont," his voice came down the line.

"Hello, Charles. I've been doing a bit of thinking and I have come to a decision." She cleared her throat. "I take it you haven't yet found tenants for the house?"

"Not yet. Our stringent requirements mean that I've had to turn several applicants away. I do have a family coming for a viewing in a few days, though, who seem very suitable. They were able to give me a list of impeccable references."

"If it hasn't gone too far, I'd like you to cancel the viewing," Ella said. "I want to sell the house."

"Okay," he said slowly. "Are you sure about that?"

"Yes," she said. She didn't offer any explanation for her decision and allowed the silence to stretch between them.

"Fair enough," he said at last. "I can understand that. It's a tough business, and unfortunately you were hit with some of the worst challenges very early on."

"Roughly how much do you think I could get from a sale?" she asked.

"For that house in that neighborhood in this market, I think you could expect about..." He named a figure and Ella's heart thumped. That much? She could pay off the mortgage and use what was left over to settle somewhere else. Perhaps somewhere up north where property was cheaper. She could get a small flat and have a new start for herself and Tiffany with the added advantage of being miles away from here. Away from Jocelyn's awful new husband. And away from Ragnar.

Jocelyn wouldn't like it, of course, but for once, Ella wanted to think of herself.

"That sounds like a great price," she said. "Please go ahead. I'm guessing there's some paperwork I'll need to look at?"

"I'll get the process started. We have a team of solicitors whose services we recommend, but you're free to instruct your own, of course," Charles said.

"I'm happy to use your people," Ella said. "I want a quick sale. I'll even take slightly less than the listed price if it will mean getting it sold faster."

"All right, Mrs. Belmont. I'll get the ball rolling and be in touch as soon as I need your input."

"Thank you. Bye." She ended the call and put her phone on the kitchen counter. It was done. She would offload the house, the last of Neil's legacy. On Monday she would call the bank about the mortgage. They'd been very reasonable in the immediate aftermath of Neil's death, and she hoped they would agree to capitalize her arrears if she had trouble with the mortgage payments while waiting for the house to sell.

And after that, she could move far away, to a cheaper part of the country. She remembered hearing how much more affordable property was in the East Riding of Yorkshire. Perhaps she could go there. Or maybe even Wales. Some regions there were supposed to have a much lower cost of living than south-east England.

A new start. From everything. That's what she needed. She should be able to live in a modest way with her transcription earnings, especially if she was able to buy a small place with a cash purchase. She looked out the front window and her eyes caught Ragnar's house across the road. The sooner her place sold, the better.

Three hours later, Ragnar sat in his brother's kitchen, a document folder on the table between them.

"I understand your reasons, but are you absolutely sure you want to do this?" Magnus asked, his eyes fixed on his brother's face.

Ragnar nodded, holding his gaze. "Positive. I'm sorry."

They sat in silence for a moment. Ragnar could hear the soft ticking of the wall-mounted clock. His mind ran through the steps he had just taken. It was a leap of faith into the dark. He didn't know what lay below. All he knew was that he would not be able to live with himself if he didn't try.

"I won't lie; I'm really disappointed," Magnus said. He sighed. "But I get it. In your shoes, I would probably do the same thing. Good luck."

"Thanks," Ragnar said.

He stood up as Nia walked into the kitchen. She was clearly showing now, her baby bulge visible under her pale-yellow maternity dress. Her eyes on him were soft with sympathy. She knew what he and Magnus had been talking about. "I'm just about to get some lunch. Will you stay and eat with us?" she asked.

Ragnar said, "Thanks, but no. I'd better get back home and let Vanya go. She's been at my place since yesterday afternoon."

"Okay," Nia said. She laid her hand on his arm. "We'll be praying for you."

"Thanks," he said and headed to the front door.

Chapter Thirty-Two

ELLA GLANCED AT the clock. It was almost two, and her mother-in-law would be here any minute. Jocelyn wanted to spend the afternoon with Tiffany, and Ella had okayed the plan after making sure that Jarvis would not be there. She didn't want her daughter being around that man unless she was present herself.

"Tiffany, get yourself ready. Nana's coming to take you out."

"Okay. I'll just finish this," Tiffany said. She was engrossed with her felt tip pens and drawing paper. Ella knew she'd need to make room on the fridge for the latest creation.

The doorbell rang. "Just make it quick, okay?" Ella said, heading to the front door.

"Hi," Jocelyn said. She followed Ella into the apartment. "Are you ready, sweetheart? Nana has a special treat today. We're going to the soft play and trampoline park!"

Tiffany's face lit up. "Yay! I'm nearly done."

Jocelyn turned to Ella. "I meant to ask you: Jarvis is bringing a vanload of his things later on today, and I need to clear some space in the spare room so he can use it as a home office. I've got several boxes of Neil's things in there. Would you mind bringing some of them here? I don't mind letting you decide what to do with them."

Ella's heart sank. The last thing she wanted was more of Neil's stuff in her home. "How many boxes?"

"Four largish ones. They're all labeled. If you don't mind doing it while Tiffany and I are out, that would be great. Then the space will be ready for Jarvis's things."

Ella fought her irritation. "Okay, I'll clear them out." She'd clear them out, all right. She would load the boxes into her car and drive them straight to the garbage dump.

"Thank you, sweetheart," Jocelyn said, and Ella felt instantly guilty for her flash of anger.

"Okay, I'm finished with my picture," Tiffany announced.

Jocelyn walked over to inspect the child's drawing. "Aw, that's lovely! You've drawn a picture of you and your dad."

Tiffany shook her head. "That's not Dad. That's Ragnar."

Jocelyn frowned, and Ella froze mid-stride on her way to the kitchen. "I thought it was your father," Jocelyn said.

"No, Ragnar is different from Dad. See? He's smiling and playing with me." She held the picture up.

Jocelyn did not reach out for it. She pressed her lips together in a straight line. "Okay. Well, never mind. Let's get going, darling."

Tiffany skipped to the hallway and pushed her feet into her Crocs. "Ready!"

Ella asked mechanically, "Do you need the bathroom before you go?"

"No, I'm fine," Tiffany said. "Let's go, Nana."

Jocelyn shot a look at Ella then said, "Okay, sweetheart. Let's go."

They walked out, and Ella went over to the picture her daughter had been drawing. There were four figures in it, which Tiffany had labeled in her wobbly scrawl and even wobblier spelling. "Tifany, Mum, Ragnr, Sofi."

Ella's heart constricted with a mixture of pain and guilt. She'd been so busy thinking about herself that she hadn't considered how her daughter was going to cope with being separated from her best friend. Sophie had become a huge part of Tiffany's life. And Ragnar had, as well. Ella gazed at Tiffany's illustration of Ragnar. It had a massive potato head, ridiculously long legs, and it wore a grin from ear to ear.

"Ragnar is different from Dad." Her daughter's words hung in her mind.

What did Tiffany remember about Neil? As little as possible, Ella hoped. By the time Tiffany was born, Neil had been well past his early passion for Ella and was moving deeper into other, newer thrills. She closed her eyes, thinking of her own memory of her daughter's father and the things he'd done. The gentlemen's clubs with lap dancers and who knew what else. The cocaine binges with his high-flying professional friends. The gambling and six-figure credit card debt. By the time she'd found evidence of an affair, he was already on his way to Maui.

Tiffany was right. Ragnar was nothing like Neil. Ragnar may have made some mistakes, but he'd been sorry and desperate to put things right.

Ella sat down heavily on the sofa and covered her face with her hands. "God, what have I done?" she whispered. She had so many festering wounds inside from her marriage with Neil that she'd let the poison spill out and spread its contagion into her relationship with Ragnar. She'd been treating Ragnar as though he was Neil, pushing him away because of the hurt that her husband once caused.

Her prayer was a wordless cry of anguish. She had botched her relationship with an amazing man and hurt him deeply, accused him of things that only existed in her own head. She didn't know how she could fix what she'd done. And even if she could, perhaps all this showed that she was just too damaged to be with anyone. Not until she had had more time to heal and get her head straight after Neil.

Perhaps she needed to see someone professional to unpack and work through all the internal junk she was carrying. Ragnar didn't deserve to be subjected to her mess. She remembered the things she said to him and her heart wrung with fresh pain.

She jumped to her feet. She didn't want to think about this anymore. She needed to keep busy. Neil's boxes. That was it. She'd go to Jocelyn's place now and clear the boxes out. Then come back here and clean this place from top to bottom. She put on her headphones and selected a music app on her phone, setting the volume to loud. Perfect for blocking out unwanted thoughts. She picked up Jocelyn's spare keys and went into the house next door.

The boxes were easy to find. They were stacked in a corner of the guest room, labeled "Neil" with a black marker. The top box was unsealed, and Ella pulled the flap open. It seemed to be full of books and documents. A silver frame caught her eye and she pulled it out. She recognized the picture that Neil had kept on his office desk. She stared at her own face. Her much younger self smiled at the camera, heavily made up, hair worn long and straight, the way Neil had liked.

She stuffed the picture back into the box. That girl with her fake hair and fake happy face had been buried with Neil, along with her naïve hopes and dreams.

A pair of large hands caressed her waist. She spun around, heart thumping, whacking her elbow on one of the boxes. Jarvis! He grinned at her, his eyes dark. She pulled off her earphones and the loud music in her head went instantly silent. No wonder she hadn't heard him come in. She backed away until she felt the wall behind her.

"What are you doing here?"

"I was about to ask you the same thing," he purred, stepping closer and resting his palms against the wall on either side of her, boxing her in. "But it's an opportunity too good to pass up. Can't you spare a kiss for the blushing bridegroom?"

"Let me get past."

"Not until I get my kiss. It's time I got a taste of some of these charms you've been dishing out." He leaned forward. She shoved him and tried to step around him, but his hand clamped onto her wrist and he wrapped his other arm around her, pushing her against the wall and pressing his body against hers. She struggled, but his grip was like iron. His mouth lowered onto hers. She clenched her teeth together hard.

He shouted a filthy expletive and let her go, raising his hand to his lip. "You bit me!" His nostrils flared as he glared at her. "You cheap little whore."

She pulled away and scurried to the door, then turned around, standing in the hallway. "I told you to let me past. If you ever touch me again, I'm going straight to the police."

His eyes narrowed. "I was doing you a favor. Giving you a chance to be with a real man instead of a fumbling boy scout." His gaze traveled up and down her body. "Your loss."

She heard a key in the door and Jocelyn stepped into the house.

"Ella! Are you okay? What's going on here?"

Chapter Thirty-Three

ELLA STARED AT her mother-in-law. Tiffany walked in behind her grandmother. "You're... back early," Ella said.

"Yes. Unfortunately the trampoline park was booked out by a private party. I ought to have checked before going," Jocelyn said. "I thought I saw Jarvis's car in the drive. Is he here?"

Ella moved toward her daughter as Jarvis emerged from the guest bedroom, his hand on his lip.

Jocelyn rushed to his side. "Darling! What happened?"

Ella turned to Tiffany. "Sweetheart, would you go out to the back yard for a moment? Just play in the sand box for a while until it's time to go home."

She closed the door behind Tiffany, then turned to face Jocelyn and Jarvis. Jocelyn dabbed Jarvis's lip and asked again, "What happened? Did you trip?"

"I bit him."

Jocelyn spun around. "What?"

Ella looked at Jocelyn's slack-jawed face. She had spent the last five years covering up for Neil, hiding all his failings and indiscretions from his mother. She was not going to do the same thing for Jarvis. "He tried to kiss me, and I bit him."

Jocelyn's eyes whipped back and forth from Ella to Jarvis. Jarvis glared at Ella. "She completely misread the situation and overreacted. I was giving her a little peck to say hello and she went off the deep end.”

Jocelyn stood between her husband and her daughter-in-law, blinking quickly and wringing her hands. For one moment, Ella dared to hope that Jocelyn would believe her.

Finally, Jocelyn turned to Ella. “I’m sure you must have misunderstood things, sweetheart. Jarvis would never–”

Ella jabbed her finger at Jarvis. “I did not misunderstand him. You can believe what you like; it doesn’t matter to me. You’re the one who has to live with him. I’m going.”

Jocelyn’s eyes flashed. “Really, Ella. After all I’ve done for you, I think that’s an incredibly rude thing to say. We all make mistakes. I know I’m not exempt. I understand if you got things a bit wrong with Jarvis. It happens sometimes. But there’s no cause to be rude.”

Ella's body shook with anger and she gritted her teeth. She struggled to keep her voice even. "Yes, you have done a lot for Tiffany and me. You've given us a home, and I'll always be thankful for that. And that's the only reason why I'm not going to the police right now to report him for assault."

"Assault? Really, Ella." Jocelyn placed her hands on her hips.

Ella started to turn the door handle, then stopped. "And, by the way, I'm not taking those boxes. We already have everything of Neil's that we want to keep."

"I saw how this would go," Jocelyn said. Her voice turned hard. "Suddenly because you've got a fancy rich guy interested in you, you're ready to consign Neil to the dustbin. We're no longer good enough for you, is that it?"

"What?"

"You're happy to just replace Neil and let his own daughter forget who he is because you've got a new man. I never thought you would be like that, Ella. Just goes to show how wrong you can be about people."

Ella saw red. A dam burst deep inside of her and words poured out. "Wrong about people? I think you'd better take a look at yourself when it comes to getting people wrong. Start with your so-called husband who's never missed a chance to proposition me whenever your back is turned. Or your son who—" She stopped, catching a glimpse of Tiffany out of the corner of her eye.

"My son who what? How dare you say anything about Neil?"

Ella's pulse raced and her breath came quickly. She clenched her fists and fought for control. "There is plenty I could say about Neil. But I won't. There's no point. And he's my daughter's father. I'm going now before we say things we can't take back."

"I'd say it's too late for that," Jocelyn spat out. Her eyes shimmered with tears. She grabbed Jarvis's hand. "I want you to find somewhere else to stay, Ella. Get out of my house. Maybe your rich man will take you in. Hopefully you'll be a lot more loyal to him than you've been to my poor Neil."

Ella froze. She stared at Jocelyn, hardly recognizing the hostile mask on her face. She looked at Jarvis. He wore an ugly smirk. She turned around and fumbled with the door handle and called to her daughter, her voice shaking. "Tiffany, it's time to go."

Chapter Thirty-Four

ELLA CLOSED HER front door behind her, trembling as the adrenaline ebbed out of her body. She wanted to curl up into a ball and weep, but she had to hold herself together for Tiffany. Someone tapped on the door and Ella groaned. She couldn't face anyone right now.

She pulled the door open. It was Macey Travis.

"Hi, hun," Macey said. "Is this a bad time?"

Ella's laugh was bitter. "Is this a bad time? Well, let's see. You've found me in the process of flushing my life down the toilet. I broke up with Ragnar, Jarvis just tried to assault me and Jocelyn's kicking me out. It's a pretty bad time, yes."

"Oh, no," Macey said, drawing Ella into a hug. "I knew about Ragnar, because he stopped by my place last night. But I didn't know all the rest of it. Aw, hun." She held Ella tightly as her body shook with silent sobs.

Ella pulled back and took a deep breath. "No. I can't cry right now. Tiffany's here, and I need to figure out where we're going to go."

"Come stay with me," Macey said. "I've got a spare room, and you can stay as long as you need to."

"Really?"

"Absolutely," Macey said.

"Macey, you're the best!" Ella felt the tears about to come again.

Macey said, "You're shaking like a leaf. I want you to sit down and I'll make you a cup of sweet tea. I'll take Tiffany to the park so you can have a good cry, maybe lie down for a while and pack a few bags. We'll leave when we get back, all right? Then we'll have a good long talk and figure something out. It's going to be okay."

Ella nodded, tears welling up.

"Hey, Dad, it's Tiffany!" Sophie yelled.

Ragnar snapped out of his thoughts and looked at his daughter, who he was pushing on a swing at the Hatbrook Common playground. "What?"

"Tiffany just got here. I want to say hi."

Ragnar's heart thudded so loud he thought everyone in the park must have heard it. Tiffany was here. That meant Ella— he looked in the direction where Sophie was pointing and spotted Tiffany. But instead of Ella, he saw Macey's tall figure shepherding Tiffany through the gate of the playground. Macey glanced up and saw him.

Sophie jumped off the swing and ran to her friend. Ragnar stuffed his fists into his pockets and turned away. He had no wish to speak to Macey.

But heard her voice behind him. "Hi, Ragnar."

He turned around and gave her a curt nod.

"Listen, about yesterday—" she began.

"You said a lot yesterday. I'm fully aware of what you think of me, and I'd rather not hear any more."

She stared at him, then sighed. "Okay, I know I really let it rip and maybe you didn't deserve all that. I didn't realize you guys had broken up, and I'm sorry for the part I played in it."

"Wow." He looked at her for a long moment. "I wasn't expecting that."

"I know. I try to be fair, but when it comes to my friends, I go all mama bear."

Ragnar was silent. The things Macey had said still stung him to the core. But although she had flayed him with her accusations, her ripping him open had brought him face to face with himself, helped him to realize the ways he'd let Zuri and Ella down. He sighed. "You weren't completely off base. You made a lot of good points, although you have about as much finesse as a sledgehammer."

A smile tugged at the corner of her lips. He smiled back. He looked up at Sophie and Tiffany chasing each other across the playground and his smile faded. "I know I made a huge mess of things. That's completely on me."

Macey studied his face for several seconds. "Ella's at home alone right now. I don't mind staying with the girls for a while."

He stared at her, and it took a moment for her meaning to penetrate his head. He finally caught her drift. "Really? Thank you!" With quick strides, he walked toward the gate.

Chapter Thirty-Five

&LLA SAT CURLED up on her sofa, hugging her knees to her chest. She knew she ought to pack some things for herself and Tiffany, but her limbs felt heavy and she couldn't muster the mental energy to get up. The cup of tea had helped. At least she wasn't shaking anymore. But the pain in her heart was so intense, it felt almost physical, as though a giant fist was crushing her inside.

Tears stung her eyes and spilled onto her cheeks. She had believed that she and Tiffany meant something to Jocelyn. Despite her mother-in-law's self-absorption, Ella had thought that Jocelyn cared about her. But when all the chips were down, Jocelyn had made it clear how little she really valued Ella and Tiffany.

She closed her eyes. "Dear God, why has all this happened? I can't even pray for Jocelyn and Jarvis right now. I know I need to forgive them, but I just can't right now. Deal with them in your own way. Thank you that we have somewhere to go. Thank you for Macey. Please just help me do what I need to get done today."

She almost didn't hear the soft knocking on the door. She wiped her face with her hands. She didn't want to answer it.

There was another knock, then the doorbell rang. She was about to ignore it when it occurred to her that it might be Macey bringing Tiffany back. Surely they hadn't been gone more than fifteen or twenty minutes? She grabbed a tissue and swiped it across her eyes, then hurried to the door and pulled it open.

Her heart lurched when she saw Ragnar standing there, pale, a day-old growth of stubble shading his cheeks. He held a file tucked under one arm.

"Sorry for turning up unannounced. Do you have a moment?"

"Come in," she said, her voice hoarse.

Ragnar followed her into the living room. Her heart was pounding with a wild and desperate hope. Maybe despite everything, she still had a chance to make things right, to say sorry. But how could she dare ask him to take her back after all the things she'd said to him? "Listen—" she said, and at the same moment he burst out with, "Ella—"

His face reddened and he said, "Sorry. You go first."

She shook her head. "No, go ahead."

"Okay." He clenched and un-clenched his fists. "I met Macey at the playground. She told me you were here."

Ella's stomach fluttered. "Macey told you?"

"Yes. She's watching Sophie for me so I could come and talk to you. You told me last night that it was over. But I came here hoping you would give us... no, me... one more chance." He took a deep breath. "I didn't completely get it, but I think I realize now what you were saying. I've been letting my business take up so much of my time and atten-tion that I haven't been giving you enough quality time. I haven't been present for you, and that's some-thing that you need from me."

She wanted to tell him how sorry she was, but she couldn't form a coherent sentence from the jumble of words in her head.

He stepped forward and looked into her eyes, his gaze so intense that her knees felt weak. "Ella, I love you. I want to be your rock, your safe harbor. I want you to know you can lean on me and trust in me completely, and I will be there for you. I know you don't believe me, but that is the truth. And I want to show you with more than just my words." He held up the folder. "So, I talked to my brother and told him that I'm pulling out of our business deal. If it means that I'll be too busy to spend enough time building up our relationship, I'm giving it up. This is all the paperwork that shows that. Magnus has signed it, too."

He broke off and carried on, a tremor in his voice. "I want you to see that I mean what I say. I've got some funds from selling my stake of

Theta Software and what's left from Zuri's life insurance. And I'll take a regular nine-to-five job. If you want to, you can take a job and I'll stay home and be the child-minder. I'll do it if it'll show you that my heart is completely yours, if you want it."

She covered her mouth with her hands, and tears spilled onto her cheeks. Her throat was tight. She couldn't speak. She flew into his arms and buried her face in his chest. He loved her. She believed it. She knew and felt it in the core of her being. After Jarvis's attack and Jocelyn's betrayal, God had brought Ragnar back to her. Her heart overflowed and he held her tightly as she wept. Several minutes passed before she could get any words out.

"I can't believe you'd do that for me. Especially when... I'm sorry, Ragnar."

"Sorry? Darling, you don't have anything to be sorry for."

"I do. Tiffany first made me realize it." She stepped back and pointed at the picture her daughter had drawn, which still lay on the coffee table, next to Ragnar's folder. "She drew that picture of you today. And she said it wasn't her dad. She said, 'Ragnar is different from Dad.' And she was so right."

Ragnar's brows drew together. She could tell he didn't understand, so she went on. "I've been punishing you for what Neil did. I've been treating you as though you were just like him. I reacted to you as if you were him. But you're not. You're the man who's willing to give up his passion, his dream of building a business with his brother, just because I threw a tantrum. I'm speechless that you would do that. For me." She pressed her hand onto her chest. "But I'm also scared that you'll regret it. I can't let you do that."

He stepped closer to her and took hold of her hands. "You're worth it, Ella. A thousand times over. I love you. It's no struggle at all to let go of that if I know that you will be with me. Will you?"

She stepped into his arms again. As he held her, she gasped into his chest, "I didn't know how I was going to live without you."

After a long moment he said, "This is probably the most rubbish proposal ever, but I'm going to do it anyway. Ella Belmont, will you marry me?"

Through her sobs, she choked out, "Yes." When their lips met, she tasted salt. But it was the sweetest kiss she had ever known.

Epilogue

"HEY VANYA, QUIT hiding out here at the children's table. Ella's about to toss her bouquet."

Vanya Klassen looked up from her seat to see her fellow bridesmaid Macey Travis standing with one eyebrow cocked, arms akimbo. "I saw you sneaking off," Macey said. "Let's go or we'll miss our chance to catch the bouquet. I don't know about you, but I need all the help I can get so this wedding magic can rub off on me."

Vanya laughed and stood from the table where she had been hanging out with some of Ragnar and Ella's younger wedding guests. "Okay, okay, I'm coming." She turned to Tiffany and Sophie. "See you later." The girls were giddy with excitement, not only because they'd gotten to be bridesmaids for their parents, but because they were officially sisters now. The whole wedding party had been a family affair, with Magnus as the best man and Nia as maid of honor. Macey was the only non-Klassen of the bunch.

"Can we come, too, Auntie Vanya?" Sophie asked, and both girls' faces lighted up with eagerness.

Vanya laughed. "Not this time. You're a bit too young. Maybe in a few years."

"Aw!" The girls groaned, but Vanya knew they weren't really upset.

"Where's she going to throw it?" Vanya asked.

"I think they said it'd be somewhere around there," Macey said, pointing to a tall flowered arch. "Just look at them. Aren't they too cute for words?"

Ella and Ragnar stood on the other side of the arch, deep in conversation with their pastor. Vanya smiled as she watched them. She had known and liked Ragnar's first wife, and she carefully avoided making any comparisons in her own mind between Zuri and Ella. But she'd never seen her brother radiate such a glow of joy as he did now, holding Ella's hand against his heart with their fingers interlaced.

Macey continued, "No offense, but I wasn't too sure about your brother at first. I'm happy I was wrong about him."

"No offense taken," Vanya said. She'd had her own set of concerns when she'd heard that Ragnar wouldn't be working with her and

Magnus anymore. The rashness of his decision reminded her of how he'd taken off abroad after Zuri's death without telling anyone. She'd had been worried that he'd once again made a life-changing choice on impulse. But after he'd explained why he was scaling back his business plans to spend more time with his soon-to-be-wife, she supported his move. She still hoped that he would eventually come back to Nordic Wind when his family was more settled.

After getting to know Ella better, Vanya had come to love her like a sister and understood why Ragnar was nuts about her. Ella didn't hide her adoration of Ragnar, and Vanya often joked that his head was soon going to grow too big to pass through doors.

"I think they'll be just fine," Vanya said to Macey. She looked around at the guests. "I notice her former mother-in-law didn't make an appearance today."

Macey made a face. "No, she marked the invitation 'return to sender' and sent it back to Ella. I thought she'd make an effort to come, at least for her granddaughter if nothing else. But Ella says Jocelyn's frozen her out completely."

"Good thing Ragnar and Ella are making a fresh start in a new home, then," Vanya said. "The last thing you want is a hostile ex-mother-in-law living across the street." She hoped Ella would have better luck with her new in-laws, although Vanya was well aware of her own parents' failings. Thankfully, Karl Klassen didn't have any leverage over Ragnar, so the worst he could do was be his usual sardonic self. And as long as Ella never expected anything more than formal civility from Jessica Klassen, she wouldn't be disappointed.

As if on cue, Vanya sensed her mother approaching seconds before she saw her. As always, Jessica looked exquisite. Vanya well knew that maintaining that svelte gravity-defying figure, wrinkle-free complexion, and luxuriant hair was a full-time job, and her mother approached it with the dedication of a career-minded professional.

Jessica inclined her head to acknowledge Macey, then spoke to Vanya, not bothering to lower her voice. "I noticed you at the dessert table earlier, and I wanted to drop a word. You really can't afford to indulge anymore. You know what they say: eat it today, wear it tomorrow. You were barely able to pull off that dress today, as it is. I could swear you've put on five pounds since I last saw you. It's a sad fact of life, but a woman must make certain sacrifices. Especially if she's closing in on thirty and still looking for a husband."

Vanya's face burned, but her mother went on, unperturbed. "And you should also see about getting some dermal fillers done before too long. Those lines around your mouth are getting rather more severe. We need to keep on top of trouble before it starts." She raised a hand to Vanya's face and passed a thumb over her daughter's cheek while she peered into her face. "I can pass on Jacques' card to you, if you like. He's an absolute wizard with fillers, and I'd be happy to introduce you."

Jessica turned her gaze toward Ella. "Well, she does look lovely, doesn't she? Such a gorgeous complexion. Some people are born lucky. I'm glad she went for the cowl neckline. It's very flattering. Oh! There's Mrs. Coleman-Baines. I need to catch up with her. Did you know her son Derek just moved back from America? And I suspect he may still be unattached." She turned her attention back to Vanya. "Perhaps I could have the Coleman-Baines over for cocktails. Weren't you close to Derek at some point? But we'll make sure Jacques sees to those lines on your face first. Anyway, off I go. See you later, dear."

Jessica glided away to chat with her friend. Vanya wanted to disappear. With a few well-placed jabs, Jessica had obliterated her enjoyment of the day.

Macey put an arm around her shoulder. "Vanya, I know that's your mother, but with all due respect, that's a load of rubbish. You're looking absolutely beautiful today, just as you do every day."

Vanya managed a weak smile. "Thanks."

"And you definitely do not need any of that Jacques' wizardry, whoever he is."

"Haven't you ever thought about, you know, getting work done? Or at least something discreet?" Vanya asked.

Macey shook her head. "Never. Not for myself and definitely not for any man. You've got to learn to be comfortable in your own skin."

Vanya sighed. That was easy for Macey to say, stunning and self-confident as she was. Even easier without a mother for whom looks and appearances meant everything.

The music faded and the MC's voice came over the speaker. "All right people, it's time! This is a call out to all of you gorgeous single ladies, because the bride is about to throw the bouquet. Anyone who wants to be sprinkled with some fairy dust, have a bit of luck rub off on them, catch some blessings, whatever you want to call it, gather on the dance floor!"

"Come on!" Macey grabbed Vanya's hand and pulled her to the middle of the dance floor. A few other unmarried ladies joined them, giggling and blushing. Macey let go of her friend's hand and assumed the stance of a soccer goalie. "Okay, Vanya, you're on your own. I'm going to make a grab for that bouquet, and it's every girl for herself now."

Vanya laughed and the guests cheered as Ella walked in front of the group of women. "Ready, everyone?"

"Yes!" the ladies shouted.

"Okay!" Covering her eyes with one hand, Ella flung her bouquet of white and yellow roses behind her. A forest of manicured hands stretched out and Vanya was shocked as she felt the bouquet brush against her palm. She grasped it tightly and looked up. Macey had grabbed hold of the other end of the flowers in an equally firm grip.

A loud roar rose up from the guests. Vanya felt her face reddening. She let go of the flowers, but Macey pushed the bouquet back into her hand. "Go on, it's yours."

Ella came up, laughing. "Both of you caught it? That's absolutely perfect! You know what that means?" She pulled Macey and Vanya into a hug. "You're both next!"

Read Vanya's story in Lessons Learned in Love, *Book Three in the* Color-Blind Love *series, coming in November 2020.*

Lessons Learned in Love
Color-Blind Love Book 3

Vanya has never felt she measured up to her parents' demanding standards. So when she meets a guy who impresses her mother, and her father entrusts her with a key job in his company, it seems like things are finally turning around.

Tendo has had nothing handed to him on a silver platter. The son of a refugee, he's had to claw his way up every rung of the career ladder. But the boss's daughter is parachuted in to take the job that should have been his, and Tendo is prepared to resent the pampered princess.

Milla Holt

When Vanya and Tendo's worlds collide, sparks fly that lead them to a place neither one of them ever expected.

ABOUT THE AUTHOR

I write fiction that reflects my Christian faith. I love happy endings, heroes and heroines who discover sometimes hard but always vital truths, and stories that uplift and encourage.

My family and I live in the east of England, where we enjoy rambling in the countryside, reading good books and making up silly lyrics to our favorite songs.

www.millaholt.com

www.ingramcontent.com/pod-product-compliance
Lightning Source LLC
Chambersburg PA
CBHW030829200726
48286CB00019B/1514